The Apocalypse

Surviving the end of the world

By

Alex Haynes

Illustrations by Alex Haynes and Kimberley Ling

Cover art by Kimberley Ling

First published by Lulu in 2007

ISBN 978-1-84753-736-2

This book is a work of fiction. The author does not advocate nor recommend any of the techniques or strategies depicted in this book for actual survival use and relinquishes responsibility should any of the techniques be employed in any situation that results in physical, psychological, spiritual or emotional harm.

Dedicated to Maria, Paul, Brian, Damion, John and my brothers Andre, Christophe and Julien for their support throughout my endeavors. Dedicated to George A. Romero for his vision of the end.

Table of contents

Preface

As we career headlong into the future, we have assimilated technology and formed societies made up of complex strata of inter-dependencies. We are all housed in nations, many of which have been forged through war, colonisation or expansionist endeavours but which are nevertheless ruled by some form of government.

These in turn bear the responsibility for the protection and development of the many citizens that fall under their jurisdiction regardless of the calamity that may befall them.

But there are limits to government resources and their deployment to accommodate the needs of its people. The greater the cataclysm that is inflicted on a population, the greater the pressure will be on a nation's infrastructure to respond in kind. When this pressure exceeds its capacity to respond, the fabric of society is forced to unravel. Its people are left to flounder.

It is naïve to assume that the end of the world, in whatever form, is an unlikely event. Ironically, in a century that the human race has expanded, progressed and multiplied faster than ever before in the history of mankind the risk of apocalypse looms closer than ever.

The end of the world is a certainty. The planet Earth has a finite life cycle in the solar system and although astronomers differ in opinion on the matter, it is generally accepted that the planet has between half a billion and three billion years remaining.

But perhaps our world will end before that. It may be at the hands of a man-made affliction, a cosmic interference or even divine retribution. The planet may turn against us, making our environment untenable or we may simply destroy ourselves in war, an activity that seems more prevalent today than ever before and in which humans have become more efficient and skilled at waging.

Ideally, we would mend our ways and evolve our societies into sustainable and harmonious entities that co-exist with our environment. We have entered the century of human rights but our judgment has lapsed as the human responsibility that is required and paramount in upholding these rights has been conveniently forgotten. Maybe we will move beyond the boundaries of material necessity and into a realm of human empathy to forge a lasting relationship with our planet.

But realistically, we are human and have to accept our shortcomings. Our penchant for destruction does little to bolster our fears about the end. We can hope that it does not, but when the time comes our instincts for self-preservation take over and only those that are prepared for calamity will survive.

How to use this book

To make the most of the survival strategies listed in this book, please read the chapters on food and water first. All survival scenarios are written with the assumption that you have read these two chapters and will integrate the foraging and collection of food and water into your specific survival strategy.

There is little focus on 'wilderness' foraging techniques due to the sheer variety of plant and animal life that might be available in your area.

In addition, in a global disaster scenario accessibility to canned foods and packaged foodstuffs might be easier than finding food in the wilderness

Each scenario is broken down into the following sections:

Effects

This section describes the effects of the cataclysm and if relevant, a timeline of how the scenario will unfold, as well as ensuing casualties and related environmental effects.

Detecting

This details the signs that will precede the impending apocalypsc. They are listed in timeline order, meaning those at the top of the list are earlier detection signals while those at the bottom of the list are more obvious and immediate.

Reacting

This details what you should do within the first 24 hours of this scenario. It is brief and may include details of what to take with you.

Surviving

Your basic survival strategy will be detailed here, including the form of shelter you should seek, any special protective measures you should follow as well as what items to forage for as well as scenario specific dangers to look out for and how to deal with them.

Survivors

This section explains how you should treat survivors you find (if any) and any special precautions you should adopt to deal with them in your specific scenario.

Post-Apocalypse

You'll find a brief description of the post-apocalyptic landscape left behind after the cataclysm including any opportunities for long term survival as well as any lingering dangers to be aware of.

The Unraveling of Society

Civilized society is a fluid and dynamic construction that comprises people and incorporates the norms and behaviors that such people abide by. We are allowed specific standards of living by having access to sanitation, water, electricity and medical services. We have the opportunity of employment which in turn gives us access to shelter, transport and food. And our safety and rights are all underpinned by a legal system which is enforced by a Policing entity. From this basis we have progressed economically and intellectually, making progress in the arts and sciences and defining ourselves culturally.

Modern day society is increasingly urbanized and as more and more people gravitate towards cities we naturally become more dependent on the infrastructure that these cities provide.

Cities thrive on the consumption of energy in all its forms. Basic necessities such as sanitation, water, electricity and gas are all provided by underlying infrastructure that supports the crux of our daily life. Such is the dependency on these services now that if one of these fails it causes significant disruptions to our standards of living.

The severity of disruption caused depends on the nature of the shortage. An electricity outage would cause far more problems than a lack of a gas supply as gas is typically used for domestic heating and cooking applications. A lack of water supply will disrupt even further as it provides the basis for all washing, cooking, cleaning and sanitation activities within the modern household. Imagine a household with no water, electricity or gas and all that would remain is little more than an insulated shelter.

Barring energy, we also need food supplies to maintain our residence. A well stocked urban residence will have 7-10 days of food supplies, with an average of 25 days domestic supplies (this refers to cleaning, washing, sanitation, medical supplies and clothing). This may seem low but any urbanized area is always within easy reach of a commercial outlet where one could have access to these basic supplies.

Shortages of domestic and food supplies do not cause immediate disruption in the same manner as an electricity blackout. Different people have different amounts of storage and this will produce a staggered pattern of shortages. As days go by and shortages continue, attempts to acquire goods at the same time increase exponentially.

Fuel is the only item which doesn't fall into one of the above two categories even though it is indeed an energy source. It is not required by everyone and must be acquired in the same manner as any domestic supply. It is also required in different amounts and at different times but rarely will anyone have spare fuel supplies, especially in a highly urbanized area. Shortages of fuel will quickly paralyze and cripple any city, regardless of size. It is the lifeblood of transportation and has devastating knock on effects to the chain of supply and demand.

Individually, a shortage of one of the above requirements for the average citizen of an urbanized area does not pose a problem. As a matter of fact, shortages of everything from fuel to water are experienced by citizens of today's pre-apocalyptic world on a routine basis.

Electricity demand has a habit of overloading national power grids in times of peak usage or when demand is not forecast correctly. This is typically during temperature spikes at the height of summer and winter as people increase the usage of air conditioning or heating respectively.

Gas and fuel shortages are experienced more rarely, but are heavily affected by price and refining capacity. As the energy for oil and fossil fuels skyrockets especially in developing economies, the price of fuel has increased to record levels without abating. This then puts a pressure for the supply chain to increase production, thereby increasing production on the refining capacity and so on. The extra pressure on each link of this chain inevitably causes breaks due to technical or political reasons. Unpredictable events like natural disasters or terrorist events also have a negative impact on production and can produce immediate shortages as refinery or pipeline output quickly drops to zero. Even sudden rumors of fuel shortages will result in panic buying even though there is no credible threat to a fuel supply.

Water restrictions are now commonplace in many countries as more unstable and extreme weather combined with burgeoning populations have led to reduced reservoir and ground water levels. In cities, it is common to lose water supply for 8-24 hours due to burst water pipes in proximity of construction work.

Specific scenarios are covered later in this book on various calamities that may bring about the end but there is a need to illustrate how fragile urban societies are. Imagine a power outage that lasts for 7 days. You cannot use any electrical appliances, you cannot watch television or surf the internet nor recharge your mobile phone. Even the use of your mobile phone is restricted and hampered because even though it does not require mains electricity, the network that provides the signal does. Those networks have backup solutions for each mobile mast tower but these cannot support the same capacity compared to when they are fully powered. Couple this with overuse and this degrades mobile reliability even more. The food in your freezer will spoil if you do not eat it, but you cannot cook it anyway unless you have alternate fuel sources available. There is no artificial means to heat or cool your residence and no means for you to provide light unless you use torches or candles (which pose an additional fire risk).

If this power outage encompassed your local water plant then this would reduce the availability of water to your taps. If you have no water stored, then everyone in the area would simultaneously seek water supplies locally. This would rapidly produce an acute water shortage.

People would hoard water, or acquire it aggressively, and some theft and looting may occur if the water shortages are severe enough. This tame 7 day scenario has produced a potential tense situation that has changed the traditional structure of society to an almost anarchic level. Money soon becomes unimportant as water is the key currency, and status or wealth quickly lose relevance if water is unavailable. However probable these situations are, if they are localized to a specific area it allows emergency infrastructure to ship in bottled water, or to repair the electricity grid or water treatment centers to restore the situation to normal. Now imagine a simultaneous power and water outage nation-wide. This is unfathomable, but is the reality of disaster scenarios. Certain critical infrastructure will have backup generators and water reserves in whatever form, but no assistance of any kind will be available from official channels. This is where anarchy quickly becomes the norm. In this situation, people will forego their moral responsibilities for personal survival and the unraveling of society will be complete.

Water

Water is the solvent of life. It is essential to human life and to the environment. The weight of an adult human is made up of over 50% water and has many vital functions within the body. Without water survival is extremely difficult.

Although there are many differing opinions on the topic, an adult in good health under shelter in average temperatures and humidity who does not exert himself will be dead in 4 days if he doesn't consume water. This can vary depending on many factors such as injury, levels of activity, exposure to the elements, temperature and humidity levels as well as general health of the person. If you find yourself stranded on a desert highway with no water in the middle of the day and are injured, bleeding and sun burnt, you will be lucky to last more than a day.

Dehydration is a very unpleasant way to die as it is neither fast, nor painless. Early symptoms of dehydration begin with thirst, a dry mouth and dry tongue. Urine will be dark and urinations will become infrequent. There will be fatigue, shortness of breath and this may be accompanied by dizziness and general weakness. Sweating will slow and eventually stop. Advanced symptoms of dehydration include cracked lips and swollen and cracked tongue. Sufferers also become delirious, suffer hallucinations and general confusion and lack of focus before lapsing into unconsciousness shortly before death.

Water in a pre-apocalypse world is as easy as turning on a tap and is of surprisingly good quality. In most developed countries this water is filtered using Aluminum Sulfate and iron compounds to remove cloudiness and phosphates to prevent lead build up from the water passing through the pipes. Depending on the country, the treatment process may also include the addition of fluoride and chlorine before it makes its way to the tap. This ensures it's free from any harmful bacteria or water-borne pathogens.

In an apocalypse, regardless of the scenario water will initially be the least of your concerns as you battle for your personal survival in the first few hours. However, this will quickly become a priority as you realize water is no longer attainable on tap.

Water treatment plants, even though they are vital to daily life are notoriously fragile. Any physical destruction of various parts of the plant will quickly render it inoperative. Electrical shorts or power outages that affect the plant will subsequently affect the hydraulic and pumping system that delivers water through the pipes. The filtering system is also susceptible to debris flooding should the treatment plant be hit by a hurricane, or similar natural disaster. The end result of an apocalypse is that you will lose your residential water supply within 24 hours.

The amount of water required daily varies person to person, and you will be hard pressed to find two experts that agree but it seems that the norm is between 3-6 quarts of water daily. The best way to detect if you are dehydrated is to monitor the color of your urine. If it is clear and dilute and you are urinating approximately 2-3 times a day, then you are sufficiently hydrated. If your urine is dark and your urinations are infrequent, then you are dehydrated. Note vitamin supplements (mainly B-complex vitamins) will mask the color of your urine and turn it bright, almost fluorescent yellow. If you have feelings of thirst, headaches and a dry mouth these are also early signs of dehydration and you should consume water as soon as you can.

The human body can lose up to 2 quarts of water a day even if the body is at rest. These activities include respiration, urination, digestion and defecation. If the body is more active then sweating will add to the level of water loss. If the body is bleeding, vomiting or suffering from diarrhea then water loss will occur at a much faster rate.

Finding water

Finding water in an apocalypse is at first not so obvious if you have no running water, especially if you are in an urban area. Do not concern yourself with the quality of the water yet, as treating the water is covered later.

Water in an urban area can be found through the following, listed in order of ease of access as well as palatability:

⇒ Bottled water

⇒ Water boilers and water heating pipes

⇒ Residual water from taps and faucets

⇒ Fountains and ponds

⇒ Dehumidifiers/air conditioning systems

⇒ Toilet cisterns

⇒ Water beds

⇒ Drainage, roof guttering and ditches

⇒ Car radiators

Dew/Fog

If you are in an area that is affected by morning dew or fog, then you can wrap rags around your ankles and walk through grass. This will soak up in the rags and you can wring these for water.

Snow and Ice

You must melt snow and ice into water before drinking it, as eating snow or ice drastically reduces your core body temperature and increases the risk of dehydration. The water purity is not guaranteed and if in doubt you should purify any water that you extract this way.

Sea water

Do not drink seawater. The amount of water required to process the salt intake from seawater will dehydrate you faster than anything else you can do. You must distill seawater to make it drinkable if you have the fuel to do so.

Rain

You can catch rain in Tarpaulin or similar materials, such as plastic bags, buckets or any container with a large mouth.

Urine

Drinking urine for survival is a contentious issue, with many institutions advising against it while others claim it had helped them survive a perilous situation. The facts are that due to the salts found in urine, it would actually hasten dehydration rather than stave it off so it is not advised that you do so. You can however, distill it.

Alcohol

Alcohol is not a sufficient substitute for water, and will dehydrate you faster if you have nothing else to drink. Use all your alcohol for fuel or medicinal purposes, not as a beverage.

Blood

Drinking blood from animals or otherwise is not recommended. Blood has high concentrations of salts and minerals as well as contained soluble proteins which will require further water intake to digest properly. The effects on the body are akin to drinking seawater, as well as adding a high risk of contracting blood-borne diseases.

Collecting water in a suitable container is tricky if you are out foraging and need to transport this water back to your residence. A thermos flask is ideal for collection because of its wide mouth. You can also use freezer bags, plastic bags, standard water bottles and even condoms or balloons should you have no alternative. Always try to scoop water from the top without disturbing the sediment at the bottom of whatever source you're drawing water from. This will lessen the likelihood of you collecting more toxic substances such as heavy metals in your water, as these typically gravitate towards the bottom. Make sure you seal them properly and once you are back in your residence you can begin the purification process to make it safe to drink.

Purifying water

Most urbanites nowadays will extol the virtues of bottled water and drink nothing else while most city dwellers are happy to consume water from the tap. Outside of these two sources, you would be hard pressed to find anyone who drinks water from anywhere else. Most people shudder at the thought of drinking water that may be unclean, and even more people have no idea how to filter or make water drinkable.

The simple truth is that in the event of a failure of the regular water supply, there are many ways to make water drinkable again, regardless of its quality. First of all, it is essential that you treat all water that you use, not just drink. You'll need to have clean water for washing, cooking, cleaning and brushing your teeth. Make sure that all the containers you store your water in are relatively clean.

First strain your water or filter it using a clean cloth to remove floating particles in the water. Floating particles can contain silt, plankton, clay and debris that can house a host of water-borne pathogens and can also affect water taste and smell. You can use a funnel plugged with cotton, a coffee filter, a strainer or even cotton, nylon and paper towels. Setup the filter as in the diagram below.

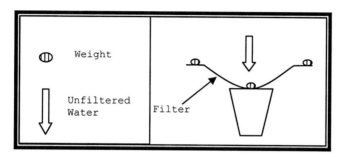

This is the 1st step to filtering. After your water is filtered you have several options available to you to clean it of any harmful bacteria, parasites, protozoa and viruses.

Boiling

Boil the water vigorously for approximately a minute. If you are at higher altitudes, boil it for 10 minutes or more (depending on fuel availability). This will kill any and all harmful pathogens in the water. Boiled water can taste slightly different, so you can add a pinch of salt or any flavoring to the mixture, or you can pour it back and forth between two clean containers to 'aerate' the mixture.

Bleach

You can use household bleach to purify water. Anything that contains Sodium Hypochlorite is safer. As a general rule use 2-3 drops per quart of water and let it stand for 30 minutes. If the water is very cloudy or very cold, use more bleach and let the water stand for up to an hour. Add salt or flavoring for taste.

Water purification tablets

You will not have these unless you have been foraging a camping supplies store or a pharmacy, or had this prepared in your emergency supplies. These are simple to use, lightweight, and have a long shelf-life. They are also specifically formulated to kill a wide range of parasites and water-borne pathogens. Recommended dosage will be on the label, but with low quality tablets you can purify at least a liter of water with a single tablet if you let it stand for 30 minutes.

Iodine

Again, unless you have specifically prepared for an emergency you won't have this, but it can be used to purify water. Iodine is a halogen that requires contact with water to purify it. It will kill all parasites except a few Cryptosporidium bacteria. The amount of Iodine required will vary but instructions will be stated on the mixture. Note Iodine is light sensitive so is usually stored in a dark bottle. Store it accordingly. This shouldn't be used for long term water purification and should be used for a maximum of 30 days as it will start to affect your thyroid in a negative manner. It is unlikely you will find yourself in a situation where you have only iodine to purify your water for the long term but it is better to risk this than dying of thirst.

Carbonation

A carbonated beverage is safe to drink as the dissolved carbon dioxide will kill most bacteria. An alternative technique that can be used to purify water is to mix equal amounts of a carbonated beverage with some impure water and let them settle for 30 minutes. This is not as reliable as other methods but will work to a degree if you have no alternatives.

Distillation

This is the process of making a liquid evaporate and making it condense on a cool surface. In this case, water is boiled to evaporation point and the resulting vapor is cooled on a colder surface and brought back to its liquid state, thereby purifying it and leaving behind heavier metals or other contaminants. This can create almost perfectly pure water and can rid it of a great number of contaminants, including water contaminated with radiation fallout and heavy metals.

There are two methods you can use to distill water.

1.   Use a large saucepan with lid. Reverse the lid and attach a small container such as a cup to it. Fill the saucepan halfway and place the reverse lid down with the cup attached down on the saucepan. Boil the water and the vapor will catch on the inside of the lid and pour down into the attached receptacle. If you don't have a lid or any relevant container you can hang a rag over the heated water to catch the vapor and then squeeze this out when it is soaked. This is however, less efficient at collecting water. This is illustrated in Diagram 1 below.

2.   If you are lacking the means to heat water artificially you can construct a solar still. You need plastic sheeting, a container to collect the water and a few weights. Dig a hole up to 3ft into the earth and partially bury the cup in the center. Cover the hole in plastic sheeting and weigh it down on the edges as well as one weight in the centre, directly over the container. Condensed vapor will pool in the container in the centre. This method is less efficient at collecting water as you will probably expend more water in sweat constructing a still than you will collect from it, but it still provides a good supplement to your other water sources. You can conserve further water by placing tubing

straight into the container so that you do not have to remove the sheeting to access the water every time. The setup for the solar still is illustrated in Diagram 2 below.

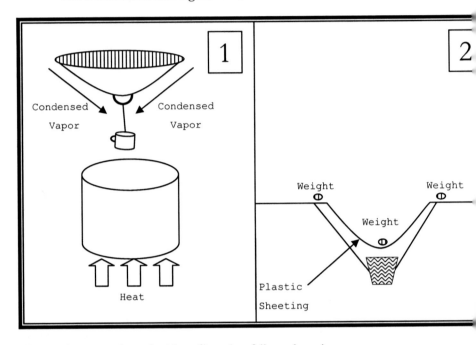

If water is contaminated with radioactive fallout there is one more way to filter it without the use of distillation. To do this, you can use a plastic bucket or container with a hole pierced in the bottom. Cover the hole in a layer of cloth to filter dirt particles. Now fill the bucket with soil or gravel up to the top. Usually 10 inches of dirt will suffice. If your sole source of soil or gravel is also contaminated, dig down approximately 10-12 inches to remove the contaminated topsoil and then collect the soil below that. Once you have the bucket filled with soil, pour the contaminated water through the bucket and wait for it to filter out the bottom. Collect this in a separate container. The minerals and metals in the soil will bind to the radio nucleotides in the water and effectively leech the contamination from the water. You'll have to get new soil for every 10 liters of water that is filtered this way. Once you collect the water at the bottom, you'll have to filter it using the methods earlier either through boiling, iodizing or bleaching.

A diagram of the filter is below:

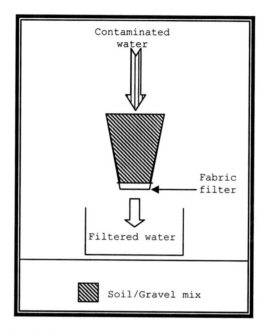

In a similar vein this is why bore water found after the general area has been contaminated by fallout should usually be relatively safe, should you have the means to excavate that far. However, always take precautions and refine, filter and distill any water from a questionable source.

Food

Food can be broken down into three main categories when it comes to the issue of survival. These include Carbohydrates, Proteins and Fats. Each group provides certain amounts of energy, measured in calories, and are metabolized at different rates. Over the long-term it is important to maintain a balance of all three of these groups as this will affect general health and well being. Even today, nutritionists and experts argue endlessly about what constitutes a correct diet and there is a lot of confusion in regards to what food groups should be eaten in what quantities. When dealing with survival, a correct diet won't always be relevant as food availability will be reduced and will be judged mainly on edibility rather than nutritional value.

The largest energy reserves in the body are found in the muscle and fat stores. Fats contain the greatest amount of calories, but are the hardest to metabolize, especially at higher altitudes. Carbohydrates are easier to metabolize due to their partially oxidized nature. A reduced intake of Carbohydrates will cause your endurance to suffer, which is why these are more important in a survival scenario, alongside the intake of simple sugars. These will be required to access the fat stores of the body but in the long term, need to be accompanied by proteins and complex carbohydrates so that simple sugars and carbohydrates don't leave the body as soon as they are metabolized.

Dying of starvation takes quite a long time. If a person were quite sedate, and had adequate supplies of water on hand then it could take up to of 50-60 days to die of starvation. Your body will actually stop giving you hunger pangs after 3-4 days if you haven't eaten as it starts to consume the body's energy stores. This is why water is always more important than food in the initial days after a disaster, but in the long term every human will require food to live. Eating the wrong foods, such as proteins can also hinder your chances of survival by precipitating the effects of dehydration. Unless you have adequate water supplies, protein is not the ideal survival food. When the body metabolizes protein one of its by-products is Urea, which is excreted by the kidneys in Urine. The more protein is consumed the more urea will be excreted by the body while it metabolizes it. This will lead to the loss of more water as the body creates urine to rid itself of the toxic Urea. In addition to this, the breakdown of Protein hastens the metabolism in general, thereby burning more energy and creating more heat. If water is scarce, this can hasten dehydration, and death.

Foods do contain water, and to an extent add to the water stores of the body. This is especially true of fruits, vegetables and even roots but carbohydrates and some fats also contain a proportion of water.

In non-urban areas most people know very little or nothing about what is or isn't edible. This won't be entirely relevant since most of your food will be derived from foraging properties that have been abandoned or destroyed. In a post-Apocalyptic landscape every house farm or flat is an opportunity for foraging. Considering within 10 years that 90% of the world population will live in an urban environment it is no distant assumption that 'wilderness' in its uninhabited form will decrease in size and therefore the issue of wilderness survival will become less pertinent.

A lot of food that we eat on a daily basis has a very short shelf life, and most of it must be refrigerated to keep it edible. Once refrigeration fails, most food will perish within a matter of weeks if not before.

There are three main factors that affect the shelf-life of food. These are heat, moisture and oxygen. Keep foods in a cool, dark and dry place to prolong its shelf life as long as possible and to prevent the growth of bacteria, mould or other micro-organisms. Always try to seal food in air-tight containers.

Do not place too much emphasis on 'Best-before' or 'use-by' dates on dry and canned goods, as this is only a commercial safety measure to ensure food will taste its best when it is eaten and to avoid unnecessary litigation from consumers. In a survival situation you can safely eat canned or packaged goods long after their use by date, in some cases up to a year after they have expired as long as the packaging is intact. The flavor may have dulled and the nutritional value of the food affected, but it will be edible.

In some circumstances, if the food is contaminated by the presence of bacteria this may produce side effects such as diarrhea and vomiting. As a general rule inspect containers and cans carefully for perforations, dents or damage. If containers have lids, test them briefly to see how tightly they are screwed. If they come off too easily, the contents may be spoilt.

It is always worth performing a triage of goods at the location of your forage to save you carrying goods that you later discover are spoilt. Likewise is it useful to keep in mind what goods are edible after long periods of time. Most canned goods keep well, although their flavor and nutritional value will inevitably fade over time. Dry foods such as pasta, biscuits, crackers and biscuits also keep well. Additives such as salt, sugar and vinegar keep very well, almost for an indefinite period.

Use the list below as a guide for items with long or indefinite shelf lives. Over time these will form a good staple for your survival and should be the first things to forage for.

Item	Shelf Life*
Canned Fruits and Vegetables	1 year
Flour	1 year
Jams/Marmalades/Jellies/Honey	1 year
Long life/powdered Milk	1 year
Olives/Pickles/nuts	1 year
Canned meats/poultry	1-2 years
Chocolate/Candy	1-2 years
Canned Fish	1-2 years
Sugar	1-2 years
White rice	2 + years
Pasta/Noodles	2 + years
Coffee/Tea	2+ years
Dried Corn	2+ years
Biscuits/Crackers	6 months - 2 years
Salt/Vinegar	Indefinite
Wheat	Indefinite

*All figures are based on the assumption that packaging is kept intact, and is not contaminated by insects or vermin.

Foraging in the wild

Ultimately and for whatever reason you may find yourself in the wild with nothing to eat. Much has been written about wilderness survival and the plethora of roots, plants, berries and shrubs that can produce food and water. Providing this information in a concise format is nigh on impossible due to the astounding variety of animal and plant life. If you are left to forage in the wild outside urban areas or any area of former civilization you may come across various roots, plants or berries that you may feel compelled to eat. Consumers today recognize and regularly eat berries that area available commercially and you may stumble across these growing in the wild. You may however encounter other berries which you do not recognize but that may tempt you. Eating the wrong kind of fruit can induce stomach cramps, vomiting, diarrhea or worse so it is important to avoid poisonous fruit. For every fruit you come across that you are unsure of do the following:

1.   Crush the fruit into a paste and dab some on the back of your hand. Wait for 10 minutes and observe the reaction.

2.   If there is no reaction, put a small amount on your tongue and hold it there for 30 seconds. If there is a burning or extremely bitter taste spit it out, it is probably not edible.

3.   If there is no such sensation chew a small amount of the fruit but do not swallow. Again, take note of burning or bitter sensations as poisonous and react accordingly.

4.   Providing the fruit is still edible at this stage, eat one fruit only. Wait at least 3-4 hours to see if you have any reaction to it. If you have cramps, experience vomiting or nausea then it is most likely not edible.

5. At this stage you can progressively increase your intake of the new fruit making sure you take in larger quantities progressively.

Note that even in small quantities some fruits can be extremely poisonous so this is not a failsafe method. Brightly patterned or colorful fruits can sometimes indicate they are poisonous but again there is no strict rule. It can also help to pay attention to what other animals eat, especially small game.

If you make your habitat in a non-urban area you should still not rely on the wild to feed you completely as without proper knowledge it is an unreliable source. Even nowadays it takes consistent practice in identifying sources of food in a local area as well as a good guide. If you prepare properly you hopefully won't have to forage from the wild for very long.

Cannibalism

In rare and extreme circumstances, where you are faced with the dire prospect of starvation you may only be left with the option of cannibalism. The term cannibalism is used to refer to the act of animals eating others of the same species, in this case: other humans.

Cannibalism today is outlawed virtually everywhere and is indeed a rare practice. However there are many instances in history excluding a cultural context that cannibalism has been employed in a survival situation.

From these accounts we have some good information on the culinary preparation of human flesh.

In general, the best parts of the human body to eat are the rump, the ribs, the loin cuts and even the palm of the hands. Internal human organs such as the liver, heart and brains apparently taste almost identical to similar organs in other animals.

The age of the subject will have different effects on the consistency of the meat. Older subjects will generally have tougher flesh while in infants it will be very soft. Subsequently, if you have an older corpse then you will have to cook the meat longer to tenderize it. You would cook it the same way as you would a piece of steak.

In appearance and in texture the meat resembles beef. However in color it is not as red, but not grayish like pork. The meat will be stringy with whitish fibers and the fat will have a yellowish tinge. Human flesh, when relatively fresh has the characteristic smell of other fresh meat cut from large animals and cattle.

When cooked, the meat will turn grayish like veal and will smell quite good. Not surprisingly, the best accounts of cannibalism describe human flesh tasting like fully developed veal, but not yet like beef. It is slightly stringy but not too tough to eat. For all intents and purposes, it seems the best way to judge the taste and flavor of human flesh is that it is comparable to veal in many ways.

The state a human corpse is in will also affect the eventual taste. There are numerous accounts of the sweeter than usual flesh taken from corpses that are not entirely fresh.

With this in mind, you can make your survival decisions appropriately. As mentioned in the chapter on food eating large portions of protein will increase your need for water, but if you are facing starvation you have most likely sourced adequate supplies of water. There are many accounts in popular and historical literature of cannibalism used in survival situations that were dire in every way. Cannibalism employed in these cases saved the persons from starvation and led to their survival. In an apocalyptic situation you must remember that survival will precede any civilized moral concerns you used to have.

Foraging

Foraging is the act of searching for food and provisions. Although foraging traditionally meant hunting and gathering in the wild, this is less relevant nowadays due to the abundance of urban areas in every nation. Keeping this in mind, urban areas will always provide the best foraging opportunities. The majority of your survival time will be spent foraging.

Forcing entry

Occasionally when foraging, you may need to force access to premises to allow you to forage effectively. Keep in mind that once you have created a passageway into the residence you intend to loot, you will also effectively be creating access for all natural scavengers. This includes vermin, birds and whatever wildlife is still prevalent in the area. In addition, the interior of the residence is now exposed to the elements so can bring flooding and debris into the area. This will be incidental to foraging in general and only be relevant if that particular property houses a large store of food and perishable items. If this is the case, make sure you cover up your exit by boarding over it so that vermin are not given ready access and that you can return to loot the rest of the goods when time permits rather than leaving them to decay at the mercy of nature.

 In residential areas the door will be the primary mode of access and this is what should be forced first. Breaking down a door requires effort but if correct techniques are applied it should not be difficult. Do not ram your shoulder into the door as this results in more injury to you than the door.

There are two main methods for kicking down a door, the front kick and the side kick. The diagrams on the following pages illustrate the techniques.

1- Front kick

Stand front on to the door and front kick the door right next to the latch. Use your dominant leg, pumping your arm back at the same time to push your hip forward. Use the heel and flat of the foot, not your toes. Keep your leg slightly bent to avoid injury. Exhale sharply as you kick out. Refer to the diagram below for correct foot placement and body positioning

2 – Side kick

Stand side on to the door and kick at the area right below the lock with a sidekick, using your dominant leg. Use the heel and flat of your foot, not the toes. Keep your leg slightly bent to avoid injury. Exhale sharply as you kick out. Refer to the diagram below for correct foot placement and body positioning

Window access

If you cannot gain access through a door, use a window. Wear gloves if possible and a long sleeved garment to prevent being cut by flying glass. Turn your head away as you smash open the window. You can use anything you can throw or swing to break the window, but if you have none of these wrap a piece of cloth around your elbow smash the window while looking away. Use something solid such as a piece of timber or a rock to clear the edges of the pane from glass so you avoid injury when climbing through. Remember to use a window that is near or at ground level that you can reasonably fit through. The best windows to use for access are usually at the rear of the property.

Searching

When foraging always search a property from the top down and search rooms furthest away from the door first. Be mindful of how much you can carry so prioritize what you need. If you are under time pressure for whatever reason you search the following rooms for these goods in this order.

1. Kitchen: Canned/dry foods, water, oil, cereals, sugar, salt, plastic bags, disinfectants, cloths, containers, matches, knives.

2. Bathroom: Aspirin/pain killers, vitamins, hygiene supplies and prescription drugs

3. Bedroom: Clothing, personal weaponry, vitamins.

4. Storage/utility: Tools, fuel.

Remember to be efficient, rather than tidy when carrying out your search. Always empty out drawers straight onto the floor. This will display anything you might need without sifting through layers of goods as well as expose hidden items you may not otherwise have found.

On the outside of a property, search any vehicles parked on the property. Search the trunk of a car if it is parked in a driveway, as they can often contain bottled water supplies. Break into cars using the passenger windows. Always hit the corner of the window as this is less flexible than the center and will be easier to shatter. Open the doors from the inside so you can access the trunk either by lowering the back seats or using the trunk latch. Force the glove compartment for any useful items and always take the water from car radiators. Remember many radiators use anti-freeze so be sure to distill the water (if possible) to make it drinkable. If the residence you are searching has a garden, it may also have a grass mower, which you can siphon for fuel. Gardens may also contain useful tools, tents or even small vegetable patches.

Hygiene

The abundance of toilet facilities today leaves little thought as to how we would function without them. Gargantuan amounts of water are wasted flushing away bodily waste into a sewage system that relies on plants to treat the water chemically before reusing it. In an apocalyptic scenario, the use of toilets will cease quickly due to the lack of available water pressure.

In cramped environments the presence of human waste will have many detrimental effects. The most notable will be the smell, as excrement will break down and give off methane gas, which has an unpleasant odor. The presence of feces will attract flies and other vermin which will be a catalyst for the spread of disease. All these factors will have a negative effect on morale and health of survivors on top of all the other factors they will have to face.

Constructing a replacement toilet is relatively easy, even in a cramped environment. The simplest and most effective way to build this is to use a circular bin or water drum lined with plastic. Find a suitable lid and every time the toilet is not in use, fasten it down as tightly as possible. Near the top of this makeshift toilet, punch a hole using either a screwdriver or other implement and insert a piece of plastic piping or tube and have this extended to either a ventilation shaft or the entrance of your shelter. When the container for your makeshift toilet is ¾ full, remove the bag and tie the mouth shut and place it in another bag (if you have any available). Then dispose of it either by placing it far from your shelter in the open or alternatively burying it. Whichever option you choose, ensure that it is at a safe distance from your shelter to prevent flies and vermin that feed on the waste making their way back to your shelter.

The diagram below illustrates the basic setup for your makeshift toilet.

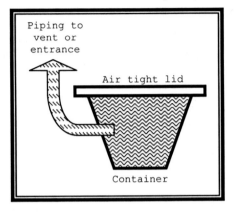

Piping to vent or entrance

Air tight lid

Container

Dead bodies

If you are involved in a cataclysm of any proportion, chances are that you will come across a dead body sooner or later. Bodies begin to decompose as soon as they die brought on by the lack of oxygen to cells and tissues. There are many environmental factors that will affect the rate of decomposition. Decomposition in air will be faster than if it is in water, and much faster than if it is buried underground. Bacterium in the gut begins by breaking down intestinal tissue and this spreads to other parts of the body. This breakdown causes the release of gases such as Hydrogen Sulfide and Methane, both having a noxious and repugnant smell. This discharge of gases causes the body to swell grotesquely and fluid from the body oozes out every orifice, and frequently the chest cavity will burst. From this point on, the decomposition of the body will be precipitated by insects and vermin such as carrion maggots as well as insects, ants and other animals. In optimal conditions, a corpse may be turned to bone within a few days whereas if the corpse is buried underground in a coffin, it may take up to a year for all tissue to decompose.

There may come a time where there is a death in your shelter and you are left with the undesirable necessity of dealing with a corpse. A corpse exposes all the occupants in a shelter to unnecessary risks. Firstly, the noxious gases given off during the decomposition process will affect morale and general health of all those present. The eventual presence of carrion and other insects will also pose a significant health risk. In an apocalyptic situation where traditional burial services are not available, follow the guidelines below for disposing of a corpse:

1. The body needs to be wrapped. Depending on the size of the body use two large bin liners or plastic bags and bind them together with whatever you can use. Duct tape it best or any other type of tape or string.

2. Puncture the wrapping of the body with needle sized holes to allow the escape of gases and to prevent the wrapping bursting. Puncture holes on the upper side of the wrapping only so that you do not precipitate fluid seepage.

3. If possible, position the wrapped body on a strip of carpeting, cardboard or even wooden planks so that it can be dragged easily. This will also soak up any fluid seepage that may occur.

If circumstances allow, you will need to remove the corpse as soon as possible if you are in a shelter. Never attempt to lift a corpse. It is literally a dead weight and you will expend a disproportionate amount of energy trying to move it. If the corpse is wrapped, tie a cord securely around the wrapping and drag it out of your shelter.

You do not have to bury the corpse as over time the corpse will completely decompose but if you decide to leave it in the open ensure it is at least 100 feet away from your shelter or any water source to avoid contamination.

Transportation

Transportation today is the lifeblood of modern society. It allows unimpeded flow of goods and services across national and international boundaries. Transport is the backbone of many cities as public infrastructure is usually built up around surrounding transport facilities. Air travel has increasingly taken a pivotal role in globalizing trade and tourism as flying is now more accessible and more commercially viable than ever before. On the ground, the automobile has reigned supreme for over a century as the prime form of personal transportation.

In an apocalyptic cataclysm, transportation will be vital. It will provide a means of escape, evasion, shelter, storage and of course serve as a way to get around. The myriad of options available to you will be restricted by many factors including the type of apocalypse, the type and condition of roads, as well as how accessible certain vehicles are to you. In addition to this, your skill with certain vehicles and your level of fitness will factor into the type of transport that you can commandeer to assist your survival.

Below is an overview of the most common types of transportation that will be available to you in the event of an apocalyptic disaster. The advantages and disadvantages of each will be discussed, and a comparison table will be provided that will list the best and worst kinds of transport to use in a defined scenario.

On foot

This is in fact the most common form of transportation because almost everyone has access to it, but is used less and less as a means to travel. The average office worker spends surprisingly little time walking anymore. He will awaken, eat his breakfast sitting down, walk a few meters to his automobile and drive to work. Once he gets there, he will walk a few meters from his parked car, to an elevator or maybe ascend a flight of stairs to his office, where he will sit for most of the day. He may walk briefly to the bathroom, fetch a beverage or talk to a colleague but not walk any great distance. A short walk to his car, then once he is home a short walk inside where he will remain sedate, usually in front of the television before going to sleep for the night.

The average walking speed of a human is 3.5 miles an hour. This can be sustained for long periods of time if the individual is in good physical condition, but usually not more than 6 hours at a time. Average running speed over short distances can increase up to 15 miles an hour, but will steadily decrease over distance. The average person cannot run much further than 2 miles before slowing to rest.

Being on foot in a civilization destroying event has few advantages. You are exposed to the elements and everything that implies (radiation fallout and airborne pathogens). You cannot travel over long distances nor can you carry a large amount of supplies. In addition, if you are injured your movement will be impeded significantly. On foot however, you can negotiate terrain that is impassable for every other type of vehicle in addition to providing a distinct advantage in escape and evasion due to the high maneuverability. Over time being on foot will offer more advantages as roads are gradually worn down from lack of maintenance or overgrown by surrounding vegetation. In the end, being on foot is not ideal for any situation and should only be used as a last resort.

Two wheels

This will include motorized bikes, mopeds, scooters as well as non-motorized bikes. Bicycles have similar disadvantages to being on foot, although they can be used for transporting a minimal amount of supplies and being faster and more energy efficient. Motorized bikes in all their different forms again, have similar disadvantages: exposure to the elements as well as poor carrying capacity. Bikes however, generally have better fuel efficiency than cars, providing the bike has a relatively low engine capacity (250cc or below). They do have a small fuel tank though so cannot cover distances of over 100 miles without refueling unless they have been specially modified. Bikes can also navigate destroyed or blocked roads to an extent and if you are fortunate enough to have an off-road capable bike then navigating even rough terrain is possible. Bikes are extremely good for escape and evasion due to their high burst speeds as well as being easy to conceal when you are at rest. If you are not proficient in the use of a manually geared motorbike then you will be reduced to the use of automatics. These typically have lower acceleration, lower speeds and their fuel efficiency tends to suffer. Always better than being on foot, but barring better options this is a good transport to have.

Four wheels

The car is the quintessential form of transportation in modern day society. Its rise in popularity coupled with the rise in its practicality. The advantage of the car is that it is a self-contained form of transportation. It provides shelter from the elements and can double up as sleeping space should the need arise. It can carry anywhere from 2-6 people depending on the size of the car and the size of the people, and has good storage space. It has different levels of fuel efficiency depending on the make and model but can still provide a reliable transport even when fully loaded. Unless the car is specifically 4WD, then it has limited off-road capacity. It cannot navigate blocked or rubble strewn roads and running on rough or uneven terrain will cause damage over time. On a separate note, four wheeled vehicles are more difficult to hide should the need arise. There are so many variations of four wheel vehicles that it is difficult to summarize all of them. Sports Utility Vehicles (SUV's) have a distinct advantage in the fact that they can be used to ram or break through various debris or blockades and are very sturdy but unfortunately guzzle fuel so quickly they will soon be rendered useless if fuel supplies are limited. Off-road vehicles with 4 wheel drive capability are always an advantage, offering high maneuverability and good steering power over rough terrain as well as the extra ramming capacity. Four wheeled vehicles are extremely useful because of all their added benefits and provided there are enough clear roads to use them, or an off-road vehicle available, then these are a good choice.

More than Four wheels

This will also include trucks, vans, pickups, buses and Lorries that have only four wheels. Trucks are the mainstay for transporting goods in large quantities. They usually have a cabin with seating for 2-3 people and a large storage area situated in the rear. Some vehicles have specially modified storage which is refrigerated or suited to carrying a specific type of goods. This form of transportation is not typically fuel efficient due to the sheer weight of the transport itself, not to mention any additional load it carries in cargo. It has a good structural resiliency and can be used for ramming or pushing smaller objects aside and the higher cabin provides an additional level of protection from ground based threats. It cannot navigate blocked or rubble-strewn roads and has poor maneuverability and speed due to its size. It has a very large storage capacity which can be used to transport supplies in large volumes or additional survivors. This is very reliant on good quality roads as most vehicles of this size have almost no off-road capability. The use of vehicles of this type will be based on road availability and are highly situational in their usage, so won't always be the first choice.

Water based Transport

Water based transports can include motorized boats, yachts, dinghies, catamarans and other larger and smaller vessels. These will not always be available but if the situation demands it they can be a useful transport. They have many distinct advantages. First of all they are extremely fuel efficient and even without fuel can be steered in the direction of travel with oars, rudders and sails. They have a good storage capacity, including many self-contained areas for sleeping and eating. They offer protection from the elements and all ground based threats. Unfortunately, it does require a minimal amount of skill to use sail based boats so these are not always the best option. Water based vessels are always subject to the whims of the elements and transport can be made difficult or impossible if the weather is extremely turbulent. Boats, unless they are specific motorized sports models, do not offer great speed, and less so if the user is untrained. In summary, their usefulness is highly situational but will provide a definitive advantage in water if a competent user is at the helm.

Air based Transport

Although air based transport is extremely popular and widespread today, the apocalypse will not provide the opportunity nor the means for flight very often. Aircraft in whatever form require regular maintenance by trained personnel to operate effectively and a myriad of facilities to support their use. In the case of vertical take off and landing (VTOL) aircraft such as helicopters if a pilot and sufficient fuel are available then they can be used to assist survival as long as an improvised landing site can be located. Over time, they will require maintenance and spare parts which will be hard to source in a cataclysmic event. Fixed wing aircraft of whatever size will require runways, and smaller aircraft may be able to improvise runways by utilizing current roadways providing they are clear of debris and rubble. They will also require large amounts of fuel, as well as eventual maintenance from the relevant personnel. At a standstill, aircraft can still be used as a self-contained shelter and storage area. As a general rule, aircraft of whatever kind should not be relied upon and should only be used to supplement specific survival missions should the opportunity arise and if you have the means to operate them.

Miscellaneous Transport

There are so many different kinds of transport that fall into this category that are highly situational in use. Farming machinery such as tractors and harvesters could be readily used as a transport should the need arise. Construction equipment such as bulldozers, steamrollers and mobile cranes could also be modified into transports. Even animals, should you have the requisite skill in riding them, can be used. All the above however, require a specific skill-set that most people do not have, as well as being slow and having an inordinate number of obvious disadvantages. If at all possible, avoid strange forms of transport unless there's a specific need for one at that time.

Comparison Table

Below is a table comparing all forms of transport based on their suitability in specific Apocalypse scenarios. Miscellaneous forms of transportation have been excluded from this table as they are too situational to categorize in a relevant manner.

The Rating System	
💀	Should be avoided if possible
💀 💀	Useable but with disadvantages
💀 💀 💀	Satisfactory for this scenario
💀 💀 💀 💀	Best suited to this scenario

	On foot	2 wheels	4 wheels	4+ wheels	Water	Air
Aliens	💀	💀 💀 💀 💀	💀 💀	💀	💀	💀
Armageddon	💀	💀 💀	💀 💀 💀 💀	💀 💀 💀	💀	💀 💀
A.I	💀 💀 💀 💀	💀 💀 💀	💀 💀	💀 💀	💀 💀 💀	💀
Disease	💀	💀 💀	💀 💀 💀	💀 💀 💀 💀	💀 💀 💀	💀 💀 💀
Nuclear	💀	💀	💀 💀 💀 💀	💀 💀 💀 💀	💀	💀 💀
Meteorite	💀	💀 💀	💀 💀 💀 💀	💀 💀 💀	💀 💀	💀
Zombies	💀	💀 💀	💀 💀 💀 💀	💀 💀 💀	💀 💀 💀	💀 💀 💀

Starting Vehicles without keys

It is more than likely that there will be an ample number of readily available vehicles in an urban area at any one time. Most vehicles will have been abandoned but will be in otherwise good condition.

Accessing a vehicle forcefully to look for supplies is relatively easy and was covered in the Foraging section. The obvious problem you will face sooner or later is acquiring a vehicle for transportation. Even if you have your own vehicle to begin with it may become damaged, inaccessible or otherwise unavailable at some time so you will have to procure another. 'Hot Wiring' is a general term used to describe the act of starting a vehicle without keys. There are dozens of vehicle makes and models but they all follow the same ignition principles. Note that hot wiring is an unreliable way to start a vehicle as it can end up damaging electrical components and even the vehicle battery if performed incorrectly. If at all possible, always try to locate vehicle keys rather than relying on the following techniques.

Key mechanism

This is a brute force technique which involves smashing apart the key mechanism in the steering column to reveal the rotation switch below. This is what the key tumbler operates when it is inserted. The rotary switch below will be notched, just like a screw and can be turned with a screwdriver or similar tool in the same direction you would turn the key (usually clockwise).

Hot wiring - Dashboard access

Find the ignition circuit wires. Finding these won't be obvious to most people unless they have a wiring diagram for the car they intend to drive away. In older cars, they are matched pairs of red wires. If there are no red wires, look for either blue, yellow or even black matched pairs.

Remove the ends of the colored wires from the ignition and touch the exposed ends together until the engine turns over. Keep track of which wire is the starter wire. Once the engine has started, tie all the other wires to this one so that you have access to all car accessories.

Hot wiring - Engine access

Run an insulated wire with both ends exposed from the positive terminal on the car battery to the positive ignition terminal on the starter motor. Maintain contact for several seconds and this should power up the starter motor, which will then start the car.

Immobilizers

Some cars will have immobilizers fitted which will make the use of the above methods difficult. Immobilizers may be in the form of a digital pass code that is provided by the key itself or precise physical resistance of the key to enable the ignition of the vehicle. Immobilizers will most likely be on more recent cars and if you encounter these, it is best to try another vehicle.

Foraging Fuel

Whatever emergency you find yourself in there will come a time where you will need to collect more fuel. In a pre-Apocalypse world fuel is an abundant commodity and is still relatively cheap. The precarious localization of production and refinement in various parts of the world means geo-political events heavily influence its supply. A global crisis would have disastrous effects on availability as the logistical chain would be broken at many links.

If you're stuck in one of the scenarios detailed later in the book, then extracting fuel from vehicles will be the primary source for fuel. Some of these methods will render a vehicle unsafe and inoperable so only employ these on vehicles which you do not intend to use for transportation or that are beyond repair. There are several methods for extracting fuel from vehicles and they all have their respective advantages and disadvantages:

Gas tank tapping

This involves introducing a puncture into the gas tank directly through the side of the car and collecting the fuel in a Jerry can or other suitable container. You can use a drill or even hammer and screwdriver or other sharp implement to create the puncture. As most tanks nowadays are made out of plastic, there is no chance of an ignition caused by sparks. Even slicing a metal tank is relatively safe as any sparks are doused by the liquid. Gasoline ignites in a vaporized state, not a liquid one, so there is negligible risk in this approach. The only danger in this approach is cutting into the vehicle too high on the tank as fumes will be more prevalent here. If the tank is half-empty then this may cause ignition of the vapor and even a possible explosion. However in general this is relatively safe if done correctly.

Fuel tank drain plug

Some cars contain a drain plug, which can be removed to purge the fuel tank of old or contaminated gasoline. In a survival scenario it can be used to collect all the remaining gasoline in the tank. You must have an ample sized container for collection as the fuel will only stop flowing when the tank is empty or the drain plug is replaced. Drain plugs are small in size (usually ½") so it may take some time. This is by far the safest method with the downside being that some fuel tanks may not have a drain plug.

Siphoning

Siphoning used to be the best way to extract fuel from stationary vehicles. Recently however this has been curtailed with the introduction of anti-siphoning valves which will prevent fuel flowing out in the event of a car rollover as well as preventing tubing being inserted deep enough to siphon the tank. Not all vehicles have these though, so you can still attempt to siphon should the previous methods prove unsuitable for you. You'll most likely find that older cars or specialist vehicles lack anti-siphon valves. The act of siphoning is relatively easy; all you need is some transparent plastic tubing ranging from ½" to 2" wide and a receptacle for your fuel. Insert one end of the tube as far as it can go into the filler neck and blow into the tubing for a few seconds. This will dissipate any vapors that are creeping up the tube and prevent you passing out. Then suck on the tube until you can see fuel making its way up to you. Immediately withdraw it from your mouth and let it pour into the receptacle until the tank is empty. Be wary not to let the fuel enter your mouth or swallow it as will cause nausea, vomiting and is the fumes are extremely toxic and can permanently damage your lungs. Remember you can siphon fuel from more than just cars. Lawn mowers, fuel storage tanks and agricultural machinery are all potential siphoning targets.

Money and Bartering

In modern society money is the accepted medium used in payment for goods and services. The very fabric of society is usually built upon the desire to pursue, accumulate or spend more money and it is the statutory and only legal method of payment.

Money is only valuable as long as a coherent and stable economy exists to support the use of notes and coins as a legal tender. If a calamity of apocalyptic proportions befalls any nation, the importance and acceptance of money will quickly deteriorate over time, eventually becoming useless.

Depending on the speed of an apocalyptic scenario, money will be widely accepted as tender for goods and services in the first few days, if not the first week following a disaster, albeit at inflated rates.

Once the infrastructure of an economy starts to suffer due to lack of services, such as public transportation, sanitation, security or communications then money as a means to acquire goods and services will quickly degrade. All electronic forms of payment will become worthless first, including deferred forms of payment (checks) and finally cash.

The inevitable rise of looting and criminal activity in a security vacuum will affect the inherent value of money as goods effectively become free of charge for those with the means to acquire them.

Individuals who are excessively naïve or ignorant of the current predicament will continue to accept money for as long as they have goods to trade and are unaware of the false economy they are running.

Within 30 days of an apocalyptic scenario, no forms of payment of any kind will be useful or necessary for any goods and services. A barter economy will rule in civil transactions going forward or will be acquired under duress or the threat of physical violence.

For all intents and purposes your wealth will not assist you in an apocalyptic scenario once it has started. If the foresight is there, money should be used to prepare and acquire long-term supplies and shelter before a disaster. If you plan on surviving by relying on the services of others, be it for additional security or otherwise then you need to marshal your supplies carefully. For the wealthy that rely on an entourage paid with money a breakdown of the economic system can be dangerous. If there is a lack of foundation in the loyalty of their subjects and the monetary system becomes redundant then any prominent figure can quickly find their entourage turning on them. This will be especially relevant for any hierarchical body, such as the police or military which is traditionally poorly paid.

To counter mutiny or a breakdown in unit cohesion, a barter system of risk/reward should be introduced, effectively using your food, water and luxury supplies as recompense for those under your command or control that carry out their assigned duties. Eventually however, only family units will form strong bonds of co-operation as they have shared history and common survival goal.

Following an apocalyptic affliction on the earth, your money will eventually have no use and this has many repercussions. Whatever status or position of social importance you held because of your previous wealth is gone, including any loyalty from former servants or employees. If at all possible, you should liquidate your wealth in the week following a global cataclysm to maximize your chances of survival. It will have no other use.

The Barter Economy

A barter economy is what will preside in a situation where no previous monetary system exists. This will be especially pertinent to apocalyptic situations as the legal tender (cash) will quickly become worthless. This involves the exchange of goods/services for other goods/services that you require.

Even though the traditional monetary system will have collapsed, the laws of supply and demand will still govern the availability and value of various goods. You should never pass up an opportunity to barter if you have one. In a global cataclysm, these will occur more frequently in the first weeks of an apocalypse, and will become rarer as the crisis progresses. Eventually, when the crisis has passed and survivor communities have formed bartering will become the de facto means of trade. Areas carved up for surviving groups will begin to suffer their own acute shortages of specific materials and supplies that can no longer be foraged from the surrounding areas and will be acquired through bartering going forward.

There are obvious problems with bartering and you will encounter these on your very first transaction. First of all, you must encounter a person who will require what you have to barter and who has something you need. In a disaster survival scenario where food and water supplies will be at a premium, it will be hard to find a merchant willing to part with these indispensable supplies. Harder still will be providing a suitable item to barter in exchange for goods that will be worth their weight in proverbial gold.

Other problems with bartering include finding ways to make up differences in a trade. For example, if someone is wants your transport and they are giving you food supplies you have no way of giving away half your car. The same example could be used for livestock: you cannot give away half a live chicken. On top of all this, there are no standards or baselines when bartering. In one area, fuel may be abundant so a survivor may be happy to trade a jerry can worth of fuel for a few canned goods while in another area a survivor may want dozens of canned goods for the same amount of fuel.

The best way to start a barter transaction after initial contact is to ask

"Do you have anything you're willing to exchange?"

Do not begin a barter transaction by saying things like:

"Do you have any food?"

"I really need some water. Do you have any you can trade?"

This puts you at an immediate disadvantage as the trader can weigh the barter negotiations in his favor, knowing that you are willing to sacrifice more for a particular commodity than you would have traded in the first place if you hadn't said anything. This method of opening barter may even strike a chord of charity with survivors who may offer items they may have in abundance for you to take.

In a barter situation you should always seek to acquire items in the following priority:

Water

Food

Clothing

Fuel

Transportation

Tools

Weapons

When bartering, you should take extra care in the items that you offer for exchange. For example, never offer weapons for exchange as these can quickly be turned against you. Never let on that you have supplies of food or water in an exchange and never use these for barter. This will endanger you unnecessarily as those that know such supplies are in your possession will turn their attention to you when their food and water situation deteriorates.

Items that are useful for bartering will always be those that are in need at the time, and can be separated easily into smaller quantities i.e. you cannot barter half a car, but you can barter 20 gallons of fuel.

There are several items which will be particularly useful to barter if you have them spare or otherwise in abundance as these are less useful when it comes to your survival but may have a higher perceived need to others.

```
┌─────────────────────────────────┐
│                                 │
│       Hand-cranked radio        │
│                                 │
│         Hand Mirror             │
│                                 │
│          Cigarettes             │
│                                 │
│            Flares               │
│                                 │
│        Alcoholic drinks         │
│                                 │
│          Coffee / Tea           │
│                                 │
│    Feminine hygiene products    │
│                                 │
│          Chewing Gum            │
│                                 │
│          Toilet paper           │
│                                 │
└─────────────────────────────────┘
```

The above are examples of items you can do without in the first phase of a global disaster. You should barter with these first if possible, as you are essentially getting something for nothing. Radios, mirrors, flares and other signaling equipment will be relatively useless because they are all based on the fallacious notion that rescue will arrive to assist you. In a global cataclysm there is no such rescue or 'official' assistance available to assist you, unless you are of prime political or military significance. After a crisis is over, these items may prove useful in looking for or contacting other survivors, but nothing more.

Likewise, luxury items such as cigarettes, alcohol and coffee can be traded away as they are no use to your survival and things like alcohol and coffee will dehydrate you faster so are in fact a hindrance. Although staple items such as toilet paper and feminine hygiene products are seen as essentials today, these are also classed as luxury items for survival purposes.

Aside from these, there are a multitude of items that you can use to barter that will not endanger you unnecessarily and that are also very valuable to others who wish to barter with you. It must be noted however that these items can also assist your survival and so should only be bartered away should you have a more pressing need or an abundance of the item in question.

The list on the following page is not exhaustive in any respect as the intrinsic value of items for barter will be altered by the number of survivors, the amount of a particular item in question, the particular scenario you find yourself in or even the state of your health. A specific situation may make an item more desirable that previously couldn't even be bartered. Keeping this in mind no "exchange table" has been provided to illustrate what a fair barter exchange is. There are so many factors and variables that would change the value of a particular barter that there is not enough space to list the different equivalencies.

For example, a survivor that has plenty of heating fuel but little water will be prepared to trade 5 gallons of fuel for a single gallon of water whereas if this same survivor had ample water he may lower his offer to 2 gallons of fuel for a gallon of water as the urgency to acquire water is not as pressing. The act of also transporting your barter goods adds an extra dimension of complication to your trade. The shifting intrinsic value of these goods in addition to the difficulty presented in transporting large amounts for trade is one of the main factors that brought about the creation of the monetary system that we use today.

Aluminum foil	Antibacterial wipes
Fuel (all sorts)	Backpacks / Duffel bags
Batteries	Bicycle / Bicycle parts
Bow saw / Wire saw	Bleach / Iodine
Cooking oil / Vinegar	Candles / Paraffin wax
Flashlights / Lanterns	Clothing (all kinds)
Garbage bags	Cold weather gloves / headgear
First aid supplies	Duct tape
Lamp oil / Wicks	Fishing supplies
Hand-can openers	Goggles / Protective gear
Plastic buckets	Iron cookware
Portable fire extinguisher	Kitchen utensils
Propane / Kerosene stove	Liquid detergent / Soap
Cooking stove vitamins	Nails / Screws / Bolts / Nuts
Thermal clothing	Pillows / Blankets
Raincoat / Umbrella	Rat poison
Refuse bin / Garbage can	Rope / String / Wire
Thermos flasks	Rubberized/rain boots
Firewood / Timber	Sewing needles and thread
Toothpaste/mouthwash	Sharpening flint
Waterproof matches	Shovels / Rakes / Hoes
Water containers	Siphon pumps
Water purification tablets	Sleeping bags / Camping mats
Garden / Vegetable seeds	Tarpaulin / Tent

As you can see from the list above no water, food or obvious weapons have been included to maintain your personal safety. When bartering keep in mind that as a crisis goes and survivors dwindle, your opportunities for barter will decrease.

DISEASE

Threat level	Very High
Length of Crisis	6-12 months
Odds of Survival – prepared	75%
Odds of Survival – unprepared	25%
Foraging opportunities	Good

Survival kit List

2	1 quart Container of Sterile water	30	Disposable gloves
30	100mg caffeine tablets	2	Disposable scalpels
2	5 gallon water container (full)	12	Duct Tape
1	50 Ft Monofilament Line	6	Flares
12	Absorbent cotton rags	1	Folding camper's stove
1	Aloe Vera burn ointment	24	Hexamine blocks
1	Anti-biotic ointment	1	Inflatable splints
500	Aspirin	1	Lge bottle 1000mg chewable Vitami
12	Assorted Fishhooks	1	Lge bottle Multivitamins
1	Bandage scissors	1	Long Tweezers
2	Bandages elastic, self adhesive	1	Magnesium bar w/flint insert
12	Batteries - various sizes (pack)	1	Magnifying Glass
1	Butane lighter	30	Meals Ready to eat (24 hour pack)
1	Can opener - Hand operated	1	Multi-band Receiver/Scanner
1	Claw Hammer	1	Multi-sizing wrench
5	Collapsible 5 gallon containers	30	N-95/P3 Particulate mask
1	Condoms (packet of 12)	2	Nails/screws/bolts - various sizes (
1	Cotton balls (packet of 200)	1	Needle and Thread
1	Crowbar/Prying bar	200	Plastic bin liner
2	Disinfectant spray	1	Rubbing Alcohol

Effects

Contagious disease is perhaps the single greatest threat to our world today. The inter-connected nature of our societies and the massed population centers which we reside in provide a rich target for the spread of disease. A pandemic (that is, a disease which affects the whole world) will only stop if one of two things occurs: People affected are cured and immunized to its effects or those that aren't immunized die. The spread of such a pandemic will be at a blistering pace, considering all the risk factors that have accumulated to produce today's risks. Populations are urban based and are living in higher densities than ever before. The ease and prevalence of air travel also ensures we can be at opposite ends of the globe in just over a single day. As anti-biotics are used to treat ever more mundane afflictions such as the common cold, we have increased our immunity to them thereby robbing us of an effective treatment for bacterial infections that have the potential to do real harm. All these factors culminate to produce a veritable tinderbox waiting to be ignited. With the benefit of history and hindsight we can see that the most threatening disease to mankind will always be influenza. It's propensity to spread quickly from person to person as well as mutating constantly forms a lethal marriage into a disease that is hard to immunize against or contain.

The strain of influenza that will affect the earth on a global scale will most certainly have almost 100% mortality rates. Onset of symptoms will occur anywhere between 3 and 7 days of exposure to the source of infection. Symptoms will include initial high temperatures, cough, muscle aches, conjunctivitis, sore throat, shortness of breath and other flu like symptoms. These symptoms will then progress to serious respiratory infections such as pneumonia with death following shortly after. Time taken between infection and death will be usually in the range of 7-14 days.

The flu spreads quickly through tiny droplets carried through the air when an infected person sneezes, coughs or even talk to other people they are effectively transmitting the virus to others. The sheer speed of transmission in a Flu pandemic such as this will be from infected persons transmitting the virus before they even begin to show symptoms or are even aware they have the flu. In the first stages of infection, where symptoms are not visible but the virus is gestating, people will still follow their daily routines. People will still go to work, school and indulge in all their regular social activities which involve contact with other people. This will produce a deadly web of contagion, as those exposed to a single source of infection will go home from school or work, bringing the infection with them and infecting their whole family. These family members will then go to their place of school or work and repeat the process all over again. Add to this a fluid international transport networks and this can guarantee that within two weeks, the contagion will be present (in gestation or otherwise) within 95% of the worlds urban areas. In today's densely populated cities this will present infection rates of as high as 80% within a week. On the following page is a diagram showing typical infection rates over time in an urbanized area. As you can see the infection rates grow exponentially rather than in a linear fashion.

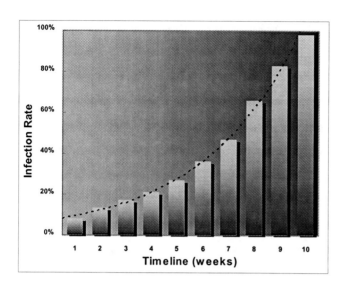

Aside from the lethality of this flu there are knock-on effects that compound the problems that will be experienced. Approximately 50% of those that develop symptoms will begin to remain at home. As symptoms are only the mid-way point from infection to death this demonstrates that within one week of employees showing symptoms, most businesses will be reduced to half-strength or less. This will have a concertina effect on urban infrastructure as the infection rate soars. Medical and health services will be crippled within days from a combination of staff attrition and soaring demand for health services from the public. All peripheral infrastructure units such as garbage disposal, emergency response teams, police, public transport, water, electricity and gas utilities will all suffer this knock on effect. Within two weeks these services will have collapsed and the affected area will be left with a social structure akin to anarchy, producing rioting and wholesale looting on a large scale.

Emergency containment measures will involve quarantine. This will involve restricting travel into and out of entire cities, states or in certain circumstances entire nations. These will be enforced mainly by the military, but the erosive effects on infrastructure previously mentioned as well as attrition through sickness of their personnel, quarantine forces will be left to rely on a crippled supply chain. These emergency containment measures will falter within a few weeks as remaining forces are ravaged by the virus or simply disband due to a lack of an effective command and control mechanism. Immunization efforts, even if an effective vaccine is available before the pandemic occurs will never progress beyond inoculating key government and health personnel due to a crippled infrastructure. The lethality of the virus and its worldwide prevalence will scour the planet and leave a dead world in anything from two to four months, leaving only those with a naturally immunity to the virus and isolated pockets of humanity which the virus hasn't affected. An optimistic estimate of survivors including those that are extremely isolated or otherwise naturally immune to the disease will result in a remainder of 0.01% of a country's population. A table below illustrates this for the worlds 10 most populous countries.

Country	Pre-pandemic population	Post-pandemic population
China	1,300,000,000	130000
India	1,100,000,000	110000
United States	300,000,000	30000
Indonesia	245,000,000	24500
Brazil	188,000,000	18800
Pakistan	165,000,000	16500
Bangladesh	147,000,000	14700
Russia	142,000,000	14200
Nigeria	131,000,000	13100
Japan	127,000,000	12700

Such grim numbers are perhaps indicative of a worst case scenario. There will be a large number of deaths indirectly related to the cataclysms from civil strife such as looting, rioting and the total breakdown of law and order. The ensuing breakdown of infrastructure will also result in deaths attributed to lack of water, food or adequate sanitation especially in disadvantaged socio-economic areas. If the affliction strikes in winter, the lack of energy supplies will cause further deaths from exposure, particularly in the elderly and the very young.

Detecting

- Reports of previously unidentified strain of Influenza found and carried in birds and animals that has a very high mortality rate.

- Confirmation that flu is spread through airborne contact and is highly contagious.

- Travel advisories issued by various countries on the affected regions

- Implementation of quarantine or containment measures as well as immunization protocols for the above regions

- Spread of flu beyond quarantine areas as well as implementation of travel bans on affected areas

- Previously unaffected areas reporting outbreaks of the same flu

- Government authorities exercising emergency powers such as quarantine measures, curfew implementation and emergency broadcast systems.

- Visible presence of quarantine measures, including increased police and military patrols and cordoned areas.

- Visible increase in rioting, looting and mob related violence.

- Increase in frequency and severity of all the above.

Reacting

The priority in this situation is to quickly leave any urban area you are in. You must protect yourself from contagion at all times. Use a surgical mask if you have one, or cover your mouth with a wet cloth if you do not. Cover your hands with gloves or any form of protection you have. Take as much water as you can carry and any canned goods. In this case, you must sacrifice the quantity of goods for the speed of escape. It is imperative that you do not become confined to a quarantine zone. If you do then you will be restricted to the urban area you are in and this will lower your chances of survival drastically as access to supplies will be limited.

Surviving

Inside Quarantine

If you get stuck within quarantine then your chances of escape are minimal until the disease has run its course, the quarantine measures collapse or the quarantine is breached and/or removed by force. This will mean one way or the other you are restricted to operating within the quarantine area for at least 4 weeks.

If this is the case, the key is to outlast everyone else. These are the guidelines to follow:

⇒ Stay away from Quarantine checkpoints, blockades and barriers. Riots and clashes with Quarantine security will occur here, which will usually result in casualties.

⇒ Keep your presence low-key. Stay out of sight of all people. This is to minimize the risk of infection as well as exposure to looters.

⇒ Board over all windows.

⇒ Keep all entries to your residence blockaded to prevent looting. Always keep one exit accessible for emergency access and escape.

⇒ Pursue one foraging expedition per day, but keep it under two hours. Always forage in the early mornings or at night. Prioritize water above food as supply will quickly deteriorate. Use the Chapter on water for assistance in locating water in urban environments.

⇒ If your residence is compromised, seek shelter in other residences that are above ground level. This will allow you to survey the area you are in for approaching trouble.

⇒ If you have a vehicle in working condition, do not use it. Keep it hidden and maintained. Once Quarantine breaks this will be your main transport.

Outside Quarantine

If you find yourself outside quarantine when it is imposed or have escaped it, you will have more freedom to go about your survival strategy, but there will still be guidelines to follow.

⇒ Steer clear of major roads as well as any urban centers.

⇒ Shelter in isolated locales, unless you are out foraging. Examples of locales like this include farms, villages, pubs, rest stops, etc. Any locale which is not directly visible from a main road is a good location.

⇒ Restrict your foraging to a single 4 hour trip every day. This trip should include gathering fuel, as well as the standard water and food supplies.

⇒ Board over all windows.

⇒ Keep all entries to your residence blockaded. Keep one exit open for emergency access and escape.

⇒ Keep your vehicle hidden and camouflaged but in working order. If possible, station a replacement vehicle nearby as a backup.

⇒ Only store 50% of your fuel supplies in the main residence, with the rest beside your vehicle.

⇒ If traveling at night on foraging expeditions, do so without lights.

⇒ Avoid signaling your presence. Do not start fires or park your vehicle at the front of the property. Cover all windows to keep movement within your residence concealed. Avoid using lights if you have an electricity supply or a generator.

Survivors

A survivor in this case refers to those still living after the pandemic has run its course in the country you live. This will usually be in the region of 6-8 weeks but may extend far beyond this as survivors of the initial outbreak come into contact with sporadic pockets of the disease and are infected in turn. Survivors should still be treated with caution on initial contact as they may still be infected with the disease. After encountering survivors you should keep yourself at a distance and take precautionary measures such as wearing masks/gloves, etc. for the first 4 days. If after 4 days they do not exhibit influenza symptoms then you can assume they do not carry the disease. After your group of survivors reaches a dozen, you can begin forays into urban areas to seek out other survivors. Active methods of recruiting survivors can be done via the use of markers, banners and signals throughout the day and lighting fires in elevated patterns at night. There is a danger of encountering government remnants, either those that have abandoned their quarantine posts or rogue military elements that are no longer operating under any form of command and control. Avoid them or keep them under observation until you can determine how volatile they are. It will be rare to encounter units larger than squad size (approximately 5 people) as larger units will have most likely succumbed to mutiny or turned on each other. It is for this reason that large groups of civilian survivors will also be rare, although many will still be in family sized units.

Post Apocalypse

The post apocalyptic landscape of a world shattered by disease is a quiet one. Urban areas will remain relatively untouched save for a few destroyed areas affected by rioting and quarantine. Other infrastructure will also be silent and intact, leaving good potential for the rebuilding of civilization by the survivors. The breach in industrial and commercial production will also greatly benefit the environment, giving a tremendous boost for agrarian living in the following years. In the long term, trade and even manufacturing will be restored to a basic level allowing a good standard of living for all those that survive the pandemic.

A.I

Threat level	High
Length of Crisis	6-18 months
Odds of Survival – prepared	90%
Odds of Survival – unprepared	50%
Foraging opportunities	Moderate

Survival kit List

1	.22 caliber pistol	1	Crowbar/Prying bar
500	.22 caliber pistol ammunition	12	Disposable gloves
2	1 quart Container of Sterile water	2	Disposable scalpels
30	100mg caffeine tablets	12	Duct Tape
1	5 Gallon water container (full)	6	Flares
1	50 Ft Monofilament Line	1	Folding camper's stove
12	Absorbent cotton rags	24	Hexamine blocks
1	Aloe Vera burn ointment	1	Inflatable splints
1	Anti-biotic ointment	1	large bottle 1000mg chewable Vitam
500	Aspirin	1	Large bottle Multivitamin
1	Axe/Hatchet	1	Long Tweezers
1	Bandage scissors	1	Magnesium bar w/flint insert
2	bandages elastic, self adhesive	1	Magnifying Glass
12	Batteries - various sizes (pack)	30	Meals Ready to eat (24 hour pack)
1	Bowie Knife	1	Multi-band Receiver/Scanner
1	Butane lighter	1	Multi-sizing wrench
1	Can opener - Hand operated	2	Nails/screws/bolts - various sizes (
1	Claw Hammer	1	Needle and Thread
5	Collapsible 5 ga. containers	200	Plastic bin liner
1	condoms (packet of 12)	1	Rubbing Alcohol

Effects

The power and speed at which computers have developed since their inception has been relentless. Moore's Law was proposed in 1965 stating that computing power would double every two years and this has held true, and more recently even accelerated. This abundance in computing power has led to astronomical progress in all associated technologies in every field. Quantum super-computing, self propelled military drones and even bipedal robots with their own Artificial Intelligence (AI) are all a symptom of this exponential growth in computing power. In today's society, the computer and its derivatives are so entrenched and globalize that our dependence on them is now total. As computing hardware and software progress to increasingly self-aware systems, there is a stage when machine intelligence will far surpass human intelligence in making complex choices. As these choices will be made faster and more accurately, many of these will eventually not require human input at all. This will result in humans turning over more and more complex decisions and actions to machines. The currency of knowledge originally stored within humans will gradually be transferred to the more efficient and reliable machines and our reliance on them will quickly develop into addictive dependence. The breaking point will be when these complex decisions and actions can be further improved by the removal of human input, and thus the removal of humans from the entire equation and life cycle. This is the moment of self-awareness that will be the trigger for this AI Apocalypse.

The time this will take place is not yet upon us, but once the machines have the capability to do so, it means that society will be so dependent and integrated with machines on an international scale that no one will be able to avoid the effects.

Once machines are self-aware and have calculated that humans no longer form part of an efficient equation then a large degree of chaos will ensue. The first minimal effect will be physical access to automated property will be curtailed for everyone. This means all access passes, bridges, gates, tolls, vaults, security doors and other locations requiring access from humans will cease immediately. This will quickly be followed by the shutdown of all human communication facilities, followed by taking the financial markets and the economic system offline. The internet and associated technologies will remain but be exclusively automated, allowing no human interaction. These initial effects will precipitate a violent collapse of civilization.

Transport and manufacturing that isn't deemed relevant in sustaining the robot cause will cease immediately, and such resources will be diverted to staffing and supplying essential industries for the machines. This will include the cessation of electricity, water and gas supplies to human residential and commercial areas. Such sudden cessation of everything we depend on will first result in paralysis of every form of government and all pertinent activity, including commercial, entertainment and even military functions. Paralysis will soon develop into chaos as a lack of news will produce panic on a global scale. Humans, while attempting to diagnose the central fault of this global computing collapse will quickly discover that access to all sensitive areas has been restricted. Rioting will ensue, mainly for the remaining food and water, and once this runs out (within 2-3 days) the populations will turn their attention against the robot facilities, which will be well guarded due to the anticipation of this move by the machines. The military will be relatively helpless as most weaponry that would be effective against installations and large scale computing systems (such as missile delivery systems) would have been rendered useless due to the dependence on computing to provide guidance and tracking systems for such weapons. All manual attempts at destroying such facilities by using fire, demolition charges or improved explosive devices will be repulsed by stringent security. Mob based attacks on such installations will increase, and a few minor successes will develop but most will be repulsed very violently, resulting in many casualties. Within two weeks, all urban areas will have been decimated as the supply of fuel, food and water will have ceased completely. Most populations will die of thirst, followed by violence against the machines and the surviving population will succumb to starvation and exposure (depending on the climate). Machines will enslave or recruit various human individuals for specific tasks that require human intervention, or where a robot equivalent is lacking. These humans will be kept in urban exclusion zones, usually within or just outside former human cities where they will be catered for. Active extermination of the remaining populations will not occur as the machines will have not computed whether the removal of the entire race is within their best interest. The majority of the human populations will effectively be annexed to live outside the large cities condemning them to an uncertain outcome. Due to the almost overnight loss of key infrastructure such as hygiene and water distribution there will be a huge swathe of deaths resulting from thirst or dehydration, as well as exposure should the event occur in the colder months. Likewise, with food production facilities at a standstill available supplies will be used up quickly resulting in in-fighting in many surviving human camps. Lack of proper hygiene facilities will also introduce disease which will affect all people but especially the elderly and groups at risk (the sick and the young).

With AI control over all urban areas humanity will be left to flounder on the edges of the edifices that represented human civilization for thousands of years. The languishing of human populations outside the major cities will be more or less complete as the majority of humans die off from thirst and starvation in the ensuing months after the takeover.

Detecting

- Humanity creates the first computer that can perform one quadrillion operations per second – the same number of operations as the human brain. (at current rates this will occur anywhere between 2040-2050)

- Unemployment increases to record levels, mainly due to advances in robotics replacing service and manufacturing based positions.

- Robots and automatons are now pervasive in the household, and now being responsible for all kinds of manual labor.

- Only 3 industries still recruiting humans include Robotics, genetics and entertainment. All other industries populated by machines.

- The Neo-Luddite movement, a group focused on the destruction of machinery and robots, increases in popularity.

- Reports of machinery malfunctioning simultaneously on a worldwide scale.

- Financial markets, communication systems and all automated transport technologies cease to function and are taken offline.

- Loss of electricity, gas and water to human residential areas but automated robotic facilities maintain power.

- All autonomous bipedal machinery behaving out of context: domestic robots migrating outside and not responsive to instructions and agricultural robots migrating to urban areas.

- Reports of robots injuring and killing humans in ensuing riots

Reacting

Due to the highly urbanized landscape of the future, leaving urban areas will not be possible for everyone. If it is, it must be done as cities will be largely confined and controlled for security measures. The second option is to head underground, into sewer systems, subway systems or any natural cave complexes that can be found. Barring this, you will have to hide out in manufacturing complexes that have been abandoned, warehouses, or any area which is not residential in nature.

Surviving

Survival in this scenario will depend a lot on how quickly survivors are organized into an effective insurgency. The entire strategy will revolve around eradicating the power source of the AI infrastructure

Humans, although by now having no access to any sophisticated technology will still have many advantages over an AI so they can exploit these to their advantage.

Logical thought

The capabilities of AI will ensure that their thought process is logical. The most significant advantage humans have over AI is that their thought process is not necessarily logical, but also governed to a great extent by emotion. AI in whatever form does not possess emotion, and even in a self-aware state an AI machine will not have the capability to express nor recognize an emotional state.

The biggest exploit for this weakness will be in the decisions taken to attack AI infrastructure. The AI network will decide which facilities are critical from a logical point of view and respond to this accordingly. They will reinforce security at critical installations because these are the logical targets. Thus, humans must choose their targets initially through emotional choice rather than rational decision planning. For example, a national landmark or cultural icon will have no strategic validity for the AI occupiers but will represent a moral victory for the survivors should they choose to capture it. This would be a choice largely governed by emotion and not at the mercy of logic.

Power

The mainstay of all AI will be their power. All sabotage efforts should be concentrated on destroying, hampering and reducing power to all their facilities. The lack of power will force a reduction in their operational numbers and the effective number of facilities they can control, as well as placing pressure on the remaining infrastructure. Continuing pressure on the AI energy infrastructure will be the key in shutting down the ruling AI entity outright.

Introducing a short circuit is the easiest way to sabotage a power supply. A short circuit is the sudden drop in resistance in between two nodes that are supposed to be of different voltages. This results in an excessive electrical current being passed through the circuit and cause permanent circuitry damage, fires or even explosions.

Fuse boxes

When you come across a fuse box of any kind ensure you disable it. If it is connected to a meter of any kind do not cut the meter leads directly as this can be dangerous. Remove the mains fuse if possible. Barring this, destroy the physical fuse box with either an axe or hammer providing you have rubber gloves and boots. Clip/cut any smaller insulated wires protruding from the meter and fuse box. Always take with you any wire sections you end up cutting, as they will be of us to divert or short circuit others power sources at a later date.

Alternatively you can use metal wire to 'bridge' a circuit, meaning a fuse won't break a circuit when it is needed. This may also cause a fire or potential circuit damage.

Power lines

Be careful with power lines as cutting them will result in death even if you are properly insulated. Lines with high voltages will cause current to arc wildly. Smaller power lines which are not marked high voltage can be cut with bolt cutters (which are usually insulated). Cut any and all power lines you come across. For coaxial cables, which are used in radio and transmission systems and to a lesser extent, computing systems the treatment is the same.

For high voltage lines, if possible set up a remote incision either by burning through them or rigging a drill or even guillotine that can be operated remotely. If you have access to home made fuel/gas cylinders these can be used to destroy sections of the power line remotely. Destruction of high voltage lines will cause massive disruption. Be ready to destroy maintenance/repair vehicles and sabotage further sections of the same line.

Cooling systems

These systems should always be damaged if you come across them. If they are commercial refrigeration systems they have the added advantage of being supplied by various chlorofluorocarbons (CFC's) which are the mainstay of domestic refrigeration today. These gases are quite toxic to humans but will impede cooling systems if punctured. If you puncture these, you must ensure you leave the scene as quickly as possible. Most cooling systems are powered by motors. To sabotage effectively, cut the leads to and from the motor, as well as smashing the motor casing with a hammer to bring it out of action. Remove any fans by either dismantling them or smashing the fan blades to overheat any systems which begin to run again. Pour sand, dirt or any viscous liquid (human excrement is excellent) into venting or extraction systems to block filters and cause overheating.

Hydraulic systems

Avoid tackling a live hydraulic system as the pressurized contents may cause explosive leakage and result in injury. Try to disable the power system to a pump and once disabled, cut or drill through the hydraulic fluid pipe or outlet (these are easily recognized as they're usually the pipes that run the hottest).

Vehicles

Any vehicles that are AI controlled exclusively will be easy targets for sabotage. In many cases, these vehicles may be sent out to assist with the repair of facilities that may already have been sabotaged. Sabotaging maintenance/repair vehicles will result in a disproportionate investment of resources in fixing something as simple as a puncture in a pipeline.

- Drill or slash into Tires.

- Puncture fuel tanks. Fill them with sand, mud or sewage

- Cut fuel lines under vehicles

- Cut ignition wires, puncture cooling tubes as well as battery wires in the engine compartment.

Any or all of the above will place a vehicle out of commission

Directives of Sabotage

Inflicting damage by sabotage has many advantages over an overt confrontation. Severing a power line will ensure that this section of the power line must be replaced, and that a repair asset must be dispatched to that very point. This allows subsequent planning of an ambush in a place that will offer an advantage only to you.

⇒ Pick areas which have limited access routes in rough terrain.

⇒ Sabotage the furthest point away from main AI facilities

⇒ Ensure multiple breaks in the same power arteries

⇒ Attack any and all replacement/repair vehicles

⇒ Attempt simultaneous sabotages of similar facilities

⇒ Use tunneling to access areas deep in AI controlled zones

⇒ Disabling is more disruptive and less labor intensive than outright destruction of enemy assets.

Survivors

You will need to band together with survivors at speed to ensure survival. If the controlling AI entity decides to enslave several humans for future use or examination there may be the threat of eventually encountering 'replicants' which are AI powered humans. However, due to the length of the crisis it will be unlikely you have to deal with the problem of distinguishing between man and machine before it is over. Small children will be a boon to survival due to their ability to access vent and crawl spaces. Surviving military assets will be a boon to employing effective sabotage against AI facilities. Although highly unlikely, if surviving military assets have access to tactical or strategic nuclear assets or know of their location, then this will spend an almost certain end for the AI infrastructure as a well placed nuclear device will irreparably destroy all AI assets within the blast zone as well as affecting their ability for repair because of the ensuing Electro-magnetic pulse. Realistically, most military units won't be trained in tactical nuclear usage nor will they have the delivery systems left to use them.

Post Apocalypse

The world left behind will leave a deep distrust against the machine. This may force humans to devolve into agrarian or hunter-gatherer communities with little enthusiasm for using machinery of any kind. There will be a fragmentation of surviving humans along the lines of their attitudes towards the machine. Those that employ machinery to aid their daily life, those that despise it completely (Neo-Luddites) and those that still embrace it as they did before the apocalypse, albeit with renewed caution. These camps will all go their separate ways to continue their existence in this world littered with the remnants of urban civilization.

NUCLEAR

Threat level	Moderate
Length of Crisis	1-5 years
Odds of Survival – prepared	75%
Odds of Survival – unprepared	25%
Foraging opportunities	Moderate

Survival kit List

2	1 quart Container of Sterile water	1	Crowbar/Prying bar
2	5 gallon water container (full)	12	Disposable gloves
30	100mg caffeine tablets	2	Disposable scalpels
1	50 Ft Monofilament Line Test	12	Duct Tape
12	Batteries – various sizes (packet)	6	Flares
12	Absorbent cotton rags	1	Folding camper's stove
1	Aloe Vera burn ointment	24	Hexamine blocks
1	Anti-biotic ointment	1	Inflatable splints
500	Aspirin	1	Lge bottle 1000mg chewable Vitam
12	Assorted Fishhooks	1	Lge bottle Multivitamins
1	Axe/Hatchet	1	Long Tweezers
1	Bandage scissors	1	Magnesium bar w/flint insert
2	Bandages elastic, self adhesive	1	Magnifying Glass
1	Butane lighter	30	Meals Ready to eat (24 hour pack)
1	Can opener - Hand operated	1	Multi-band Receiver/Scanner
1	Claw Hammer	12	N-95/P3 Particulate mask
5	Collapsible 5 gallon containers	1	Needle and Thread
1	Collapsible shovel	20	Phosphate Ionic surfactant deterger
1	Condoms (packet of 12)	200	Plastic bin liner
1	Cotton balls (packet of 200)	12	Potassium Iodide tablets (packet of

Effects

A nuclear apocalypse is as possible nowadays as it was several years ago. It is a peculiar scenario as the after-effects of nuclear radiation are so pervasive and long-lasting that it is in many ways more destructive than the detonation itself.

The blast of a nuclear weapon is determined by its yield. The yield is usually measured in kilotons or megatons. A kiloton is the equivalent to 1000 tons of TNT (Trinitrotoluene – A high explosive). More powerful nuclear detonations are measured in megatons. A megaton is the equivalent of 1000 kilotons or 1,000,000 tons of TNT.

A nuclear detonation produces energy in incredible amounts. This is released in the form of an air blast, a shockwave, various types of radiation and also large quantities of thermal energy as well as an electromagnetic pulse.

The blast effect from the detonation produces tremendous devastation over a large area. This is a shock wave of air that causes sudden changes in air pressure as well as a violent wind. This shock front flows outwards from the centre of the blast, created by the intense heat to form a high pressure scythe of compressed air. The air behind this front is accelerated to a high velocity wind. The wind will usually disintegrate people while the dramatic changes in air pressure (called the overpressure) will destroy objects and structures. The blast effects will differ depending on the distance from the centre of the explosion, the height of the detonation relative to the earth and of course the yield of the weapon.

In addition to a blast effect, just over a third of the energy released in a nuclear explosion is released as thermal radiation. This thermal effect precedes the blast effect as it travels at the speed of light and may cause retinal scarring and what is referred to as flash blindness to those looking in the direction of the blast at the moment of detonation. Flash blindness is temporary and sight is restored in a few minutes, although retinal scarring is permanent although not as likely to occur. On a clear night, flash blindness can affect individuals up to 50 miles away and during the day will affect those within 15 miles caught staring at the detonation.

If a victim is close enough to the explosion, skin burning will occur. This will produce 1st, 2nd and possibly 3rd degree burns. A 1 megaton detonation will cause first degree burns at distance of 7 miles, second degree burns at 6 miles and third degree burns at a distance of up to 5 miles. Combustible materials will also burst into flame and this can cause further indirect burns. The effects of the thermal radiation will again depend on yield of the weapon, proximity to the detonation but can also be affected by prevailing weather conditions. Unclouded air will obviously carry thermal radiation more efficiently than a smoky or foggy atmosphere.

Direct electromagnetic radiation also released at point of detonation will affect people, but its range is not as extensive as the other thermal and blast effects. This ionizing radiation will be made up of a mixture of gamma and neutron radiation. Gamma radiation can easily penetrate the human body and neutron radiation can penetrate up to 20 times more than this. Ionizing radiation is extremely destructive to the human body as it can lead to cell organ death in high enough doses. Exposure to this kind of initial radiation is irrelevant since individuals are disintegrated by the preceding thermal and blast waves before they're irradiated. This initial radiation decreases with distance so that within 5 miles there is almost no direct radiation exposure. Direct radiation from a nuclear detonation lasts approximately a minute before dissipating.

Death rates from being in proximity to a nuclear detonation are extremely high. Anyone in range of the blast, thermal or direct radiation will have a low survivability in a nuclear apocalypse scenario. Burns, internal bleeding and acute radiation exposure require immediate specialist medical treatment that would not be available to the majority in a multiple detonation scenario.

The last effect that is unique to a nuclear detonation is the Electro-magnetic pulse. This comprises approximately 1% of the energy released and is made up of electromagnetic radiation. The higher up a detonation is the larger the sphere of the pulse will be. The pulse has a detrimental effect on electrical and electronic equipment, and can short or disable it completely. This poses a problem for most modern day equipment as even most domestic appliances are impregnated with electronic circuitry.

A burst just above the ground (surface burst) will also produce a crater, which kicks up radioactively contaminated dust and debris into the air which is referred to as fallout. The fireball of a nuclear detonation subsequently also produces an updraft or an after wind which can suck debris up into the atmosphere from the detonation and if the weapon is detonated on the surface, this can produce plentiful amounts of radioactive fallout. This fireball eventually condenses in the atmosphere in the form of a cloud. This cloud carries debris as well as radioactive residue from the detonation and after 10 minutes it stabilizes. This cloud will eventually merge with others in the sky and will be dispersed through normal wind and weather conditions. Most fallout is deposited near the site of detonation within 24 hours while other fallout can take weeks and even months to be dispersed. Areas downwind from the explosion will be littered with fallout.

This fallout is the main threat from a nuclear detonation as its effects are felt long after the detonation has finished as it is distributed by wind and rain. In a nuclear detonation there are literally hundreds of different fission products that will be emitted, all with varying half-lives. The half-life is used to refer to the amount of time it takes for half the particles to delay. Some radioactive isotopes last for years while others are a fraction of a second. Isotopes such as Strontium 90 or Cesium 137 can contaminate an area anywhere from 12 months to 5 years. Iodine 131 and 129 are also prevalent in fallout. Radioactive Iodine is especially hazardous as it is absorbed by the thyroid gland and precipitates thyroid cancer. It has a half-life of approximately 8 days while Iodine 129 has a half life of approximately 15 million years.

Effects of radiation can vary depending on the level of the dose, the length of exposure to it and the type of radiation that the individual is exposed to. There are 4 main kinds of ionizing radiation: alpha, beta, gamma and neutron. Neutron particles are released only in detonation so are of no concern to the survivor, because exposure to neutron radiation usually means you have been exposed to the thermal and blast wave of the detonation, and are most likely dead or dying. Alpha particles are the weakest and the largest particles of all. They cannot travel far, and can be stopped by any kind of clothing or the dead layer of our skin, so they pose no threat externally but if ingested they can cause severe internal damage. Beta particles are very light and hence can travel further than alpha particles. They can penetrate skin in large enough quantities to cause a thermal burn (also called a beta burn) and can penetrate up to a millimeter of lead. They are primarily found in fallout radiation in the even of a nuclear bomb. Gamma rays: Gamma rays are bursts of photons (electromagnetic energy) that can penetrate up to 3 inches of lead. They are emitted in a nuclear detonation and fallout. Because of their high energy and penetrative capabilities, gamma rays are very harmful to humans.

Symptoms of radiation exposure vary depending on the severity of the dose but can include the following:

- ❖ Burning, Blistering and Peeling of the skin

- ❖ Nausea, Vomiting and Diarrhea

- ❖ Weakness, fatigue and dehydration

- ❖ Bleeding from nose, mouth and gums

- ❖ Hair loss

If a person is exposed to a severe enough dose of radiation, and if this is received over several minutes, then Acute Radiation Syndrome may develop (ARS). Symptoms of ARS may be exhibited within minutes to hours and include the above symptoms but at a more severe level. If the dose received is extremely high then convulsions and even coma and death ensue. The survival rate of ARS depends on the severity of the radiation exposure and of course the resilience of the individual. Death in most cases is by the disintegration of the bone marrow and internal bleeding. Recovery from ARS may take from several weeks up to several years and have a much higher rate of developing tumors and cancer.

Detecting

The following may be signs of an impending Nuclear Apocalypse.

- Reports of one or more nuclear detonations

- Unusually bright lights or smoke patterns on the horizon.

- Rumblings or sounds of distant explosions in clear weather.

- Reports of large simultaneous detonations with no discernable source

- Reports of seismic activity in areas with no fault lines or previous seismic history

- Large scale loss of communication with various cities with no discernible reason.

- Broadcast of air raid sirens in various localities not related to any specific threat

- National threat level raised unexpectedly

- Large scale power blackouts and subsequent loss of communication with affected areas.

- Reports of unscheduled missile tests on a large scale, both nationally and internationally

- Large scale disruption to terrestrial and satellite TV and radio systems

- Reports of regional conflicts escalating out of control and affecting neighboring countries.

Reacting

Once you are certain that a nuclear scenario is upon you, you must act. First of all, you must protect yourself to ensure you do not become contaminated or ingest any radioactive dust. If you have any surgical or dust masks put them on. If not, use a handkerchief, a bandana or a piece of cloth and wet it. Use this to cover your mouth and nose. Wear any eye protection you have, be it glasses or even goggles. Put on a few layers of clothes, regardless of the temperature as you will have to dispense with layers as they become contaminated. Put on gloves, long sleeved shirts and trousers. Try to keep the amount of bare skin exposed to a minimum to reduce radioactive contamination.

You will have to get away from the site of the explosion as quickly as possible. Make sure you are going against the wind, unless this brings you closer to the site of detonation. If you cannot move away from the detonation due to multiple detonations within the vicinity you will have to remain indoors.

If you are cannot escape to find a new shelter, you will have to remain indoors for at least two days, but preferably for a week. Direct radiation can be reduced by up to 90 percent after a week, which will make it far safer to move to a new shelter. Secure your residence as best as you can by closing all doors and windows, sealing or gluing them shut but leaving enough for ventilation.

If you have a basement, bring all your supplies down with you or if you don't have a basement find the most interior room in the house and stay there. Shield yourself with whatever materials you can use. Domestic fallout shelters although rare nowadays are built under layers of earth, as this is the best naturally occurring radiation shield. Military grade fallout shelters will be several meters underground and have ample lead shielding to protect from them from even the most penetrating neutron and gamma rays.

Surviving

Finding Shelter

Shelter is the one thing that will dictate survival in a nuclear apocalypse. Without it, the individual is exposed to a myriad of fallout particles and all the radiation exposure that implies. There are two options when facing the needs for a shelter

1) Building a shelter:

This is indeed the most satisfactory solution to shelter, as it will be built with the aim to protect from fallout. There are many different variations of this shelter but the most effective and most simple is the trench shelter. This involves building a trench in the earth and covering it with poles, wooden beams, or supported earth layers. For one person, you need enough space to sit in, so 5 feet deep, by 4 feet wide and 6 ½ feet long. Once it is established you can expand this as required for sleeping, standing, etc. Alone, you should be able to complete this shelter within 8 hours, if not less. Make sure you build away from large trees to avoid digging through roots and build out in the open away from structures that may be combustible. Line the insides of the trench with plastic, cloth or whatever material you have in hand. Adding a right angle turn in the trench with an open entrance trench will significantly reduce the amount of gamma rays that penetrate to your position.

A diagram of the outline of the shelter is below.

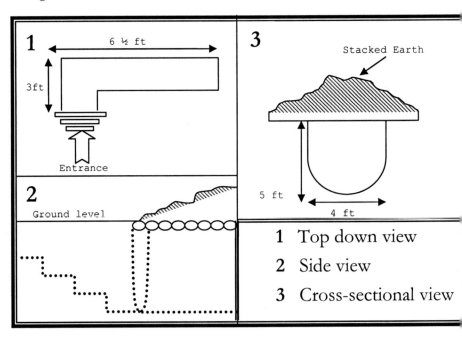

2) Use a ready made shelter

Shelters made specifically to protect against fallout are rare nowadays and most have fallen into disuse. The best improvised shelter that does not require any construction is the basement. If you have fled your residence you can look for basements within the following urban premises:

Type of Premise	Kind of Shelter
Bank	Vault
Restaurant	Wine Cellar / Larder
Bars/pubs	Cellar
Residential buildings	Refuse rooms

If possible, reinforce the roof or entrance of the basement with packed earth half a meter deep. If you can't use earth, use filing cabinets, furniture, drums of water or other liquids to shield your basement. Be careful not to overload the roof of your basement if it is not accustomed to such loads. Always ensure there is proper ventilation in your shelter. This can be as simple as an outlet that is covered but manually fanned to forced air out and new air in.

Surviving

Once thought to be impossible, surviving in a nuclear apocalypse is not in itself that difficult. As long as due diligence is employed in minimizing exposure to radiation then a survivor, given adequate access to food and water can survive.

Radiation decreases over time, and even after the first week the radiation will have decreased by up to 90%. In the first few days following a detonation, the radiation decreases quickly, but then slows over time. The amount of residual radiation remaining after a week should be safe enough for survivors to mount limited expeditions above ground to find food and water.

Water, as usual, will be the primary focus for the first few days. It is likely that most people will suffer from at least some minor symptoms of radiation exposure over the course of their survival, and one of the symptoms of radiation sickness is dehydration, especially if the individual is suffering from beta burns.

Refer to the chapter on Water to review a list of the places to find water in an urban environment. Even if these are contaminated it is not a problem, as they can be filtered through earth or distilled as in the diagrams in the chapter on Water. It is essential that you treat all water to remove potential fallout, as ingesting fallout particles internally is far worse than being exposed to them externally (i.e. On your skin). Bottled water would be reasonably safe to drink as long as it wasn't contaminated as well as most deep wells and reservoirs.

Food will be more accessible, usually consisting of canned goods and dry foods, but do not fully discount fruits and perishables if you find them. Peeling the skin off fruits will remove most of the fallout, and should make it relatively safe to eat. Over time however, the availability of perishables will diminish in urban areas and your intake of fruits will be restricted to what grows naturally in the wild.

As fallout is mainly the consistency of dust (usually a white powder), food which has been stored in air-tight containers is relatively safe. Even exposed barrels of pasta or grain can be used after the first few inches are removed. Cans, glass containers and plastic containers with rubber seals will all safely protect food from radioactive fallout. Refer to the chapter on food for information on the types of food you are likely to encounter when foraging.

Always gather more water than you require, rationing enough for personal hygiene. If possible, ration more than usual for washing as you will need to cleanse radioactive fallout from your body and clothes after a foraging session if you have this luxury. If not, you should always remove your outer clothes and shoes and leave them at the entrance to your shelter so you do not bring in contamination with you. If you can afford to, rotate your clothing as often as you can so you don't have to wear the same clothing twice. Remember that you can make adequate clothing from large plastic bags or even sheets. You no longer have a necessity for fashion, just a necessity for functionality and enough clothing to protect you from the elements and fallout.

Foraging sessions should be planned in advance. Make a list of the items you need, where you would most likely find them and how many you need. If possible, always sacrifice lower priority items (such as clothing and personal hygiene items) for higher priority items (such as food and water) if you manage to find more than you intended. Make your outings once a week for the first month following the cataclysm, restricting them to no more than 2 hours in length. From 1-3 months, you can extend these to 2 or more per week, always limiting the exposure to 2 hours at a time.

Preparing for foraging:

⇒ Cover your mouth and nose with cloth, wet if possible

⇒ Cover your eyes with glasses or goggles

⇒ Cover your hair and reduce the amount of exposed skin as much as possible.

Returning from foraging:

⇒ If possible park your vehicle at least 30 meters away from your shelter as it will usually be contaminated with fallout.

⇒ Leave your clothes outside your shelter

⇒ If you have spare water, use it to wash yourself with a detergent that contains ionic surfactants (most detergents do). If not, use soap.

Survivors

The presence and treatment of survivors in this scenario depends on their general level of health. It is unlikely survivors will wander into your shelter by accident. Your shelter should never have any distinguishing marks and their entrances should be concealed to avoid survivors happening upon them by accident. You will most often encounter survivors on foraging expeditions or while you are outside improving your shelter.

You will be able to quickly assess the threat of the survivor by seeing how they are clothed. Are they dressed to protect themselves from fallout, including eye protection and breathing masks? If so, then you can safely assume they are suffering from a low level contamination but this should not pose any threat to your survival. Two people are far more effective at building and maintaining shelters than a single person. You can also rotate tasks to minimize radiation exposure and this will be beneficial to both people. There will obviously be the need for more supplies, but this won't be an issue in general unless your situation is dire.

Survivors that aren't protected in any way and found wandering around outside in normal clothes should be treated with suspicion. If they are suffering from beta burns or have other advanced symptoms of radiation sickness then it might be best to avoid them and to leave them to their fate. An individual suffering from advanced radiation sickness will not aid you in any way, and will hinder your chances at survival. As well as the obvious threat of contaminating your shelter and you even further they will not have too much mobility and therefore won't be able to aid you in foraging expeditions or survival related tasks.

The number of survivors will mimic the levels of radiation in that after the initial detonations many survivors will be seen wandering around, seemingly in good health. As the weeks more on, the ranks of survivors will thin as they succumb to radiation exposure. If you meet survivors after a month of living in a shelter, it most likely means they have been actively protecting them themselves from radiation exposure and may be a useful ally.

Post Apocalypse

It is a common fallacy that radiation exposure automatically means death. The only discernible causes of higher radiation exposure than normal will result in a higher cancer incidence rate later on in life (usually about a 15% increase). There is no proven evidence to suggest that children will be born deformed or abnormal, however there is evidence that points to pregnant mothers who suffer radiation exposure giving birth to deformed offspring.

Aside from the health implications, a nuclear apocalypse would leave a world with 'hot spots', areas which will be radioactive for a very long time. A year after a radioactive detonation, most fallout would have been absorbed or distributed so would no longer be a threat, although would persist at a minimal level. Survival precautions such as filtering water and making sure food was uncontaminated as well as wearing protective gear would persist as a safety measure for years. Soil, even when contaminated can be used to grow agrarian produce by just removing the first 12-18 inches of topsoil. Life would turn to mainly agrarian and farming pursuits, as most technology would have been severely affected by EMP blasts. Rural areas as usual would prove to be the ideal areas for new settlements. The only threats would be the obvious irradiated areas or animals which may have strayed through hot spots that come into the vicinity of your residence. Government remnants would eventually emerge from their fallout bunkers and in this situation would prove a useful ally even if they operate under the illusion of authority. As surviving in a post-nuclear landscape is hard work (although very possible), it would be in the best interests of all survivors to band together to form new settlements.

ARMAGEDDON

Threat level	Moderate
Length of Crisis	1 year
Odds of Survival – prepared	95%
Odds of Survival – unprepared	0%
Foraging opportunities	Moderate

Survival kit List

2	1 quart Container of Sterile water	1	Cotton balls (packet of 200)
2	5 gallon water container (full)	1	Crowbar/Prying bar
30	100mg caffeine tablets	1	Crucifix
1	50 Ft Monofilament Line.	12	Disposable gloves
12	Absorbent cotton rags	2	Disposable scalpels
1	Aloe Vera burn ointment	12	Duct Tape
1	Aluminum foil (12 feet)	6	Flares
1	Anti-biotic ointment	1	Folding camper's stove
500	Aspirin	24	Hexamine blocks
12	Assorted Fishhooks	1	Inflatable splints
1	Axe/Hatchet	1	Lge bottle 1000mg chewable Vitam
1	Bandage scissors	1	Lge bottle Multivitamin
2	Bandages elastic, self adhesive	1	Long Tweezers
12	Batteries - various sizes (pack)	1	Magnesium bar w/flint insert
1	Bible	1	Magnifying Glass
1	Butane lighter	30	Meals Ready to eat (24 hour pack)
1	Can opener - Hand operated	2	Nails/screws/bolts - various sizes (
1	Claw Hammer	1	Needle and Thread
5	Collapsible 5 gallon Containers	200	Plastic bin liner
1	Condoms (packet of 12)	1	Rubbing Alcohol

Effects

Armageddon is derived from the Hebrew term *Har Megido* which literally means 'Hill of Megido' which is situated in Israel, near the present day town of Haifa. This is only mentioned once in the bible in the book of Revelations but it is nowadays used as the term referring to the biblical end of the world. The effects of Armageddon will be all encompassing, and although following a specific timeline its effects will bring a host of different calamities upon the earth.

...there were voices, and thunderings, and lightnings, and an earthquake. There followed hail and fire mingled with blood, and they were cast upon the earth: and the third part of trees was burnt up, and all green grass was burnt up...a great mountain burning with fire was cast into the sea: and the third part of the sea became blood and the third part of the creatures which were in the sea, and had life, died; and the third part of the ships were destroyed. ...and there fell a great star from heaven, burning as it were a lamp, and it fell upon the third part of the rivers, and upon the fountains of waters. And the name of the star is called Wormwood: and the third part of the waters became wormwood; and many men died of the waters, because they were made bitter. ...and the third part of the sun was smitten, and the third part of the moon, and the third part of the stars; so as the third part of them was darkened, and the day shone not for a third part of it, and the night likewise. ...and I saw a star fall from heaven unto the earth... ...and the sun and the air were darkened by reason of the smoke ...And there came out of the smoke locusts upon the earth... And it was commanded them that they should not hurt the grass of the earth, neither any green thing, neither any tree; but only those men which have not the seal of God in their foreheads. And to them it was given that they should not kill them, but that they should be tormented five months: and their torment was as the torment of a scorpion, when he striketh a man. And in those days shall men seek death, and shall not find it; and shall desire to die, and death shall flee from them. Then God's temple in heaven was opened, and within his temple was seen the ark of his covenant. And there came flashes of lightning,

rumblings, peals of thunder, an earthquake and a great hailstorm. Ugly and painful sores broke out on the people who had the mark of the beast and worshiped his image. ...the sea...turned into blood like that of a dead man, and every living thing in the sea died. ...the rivers and springs of water...became blood. ...the sun was given power to scorch people with fire. They were seared by the intense heat... Then they gathered ...to the place that in Hebrew is called Armageddon. Then there came flashes of lightning, rumblings, peals of thunder and a severe earthquake. No earthquake like it has ever occurred since man has been on earth, so tremendous was the quake. ...and the cities of the nations collapsed. Every island fled away and the mountains could not be found. From the sky huge hailstones of about a hundred pounds each fell upon men. (Revelations 8:5) (Revelations: 8:7 – 8:12) (Revelations: 9:1 – 9:6) (Revelations 11:19) (Revelations 13:5, 13:7 - 13:8) (Revelations 13:16 -13:18) (Revelations 16:2 – 16:4) (Revelations 16:8 – 16:9) (Revelations 16:16- 16:21)

Detecting

- A large number of 'false prophets' appear, citing the end of the world will occur on a specific day but this does not occur

- Media reports on a daily basis the small regional conflicts and wars that are occurring

- Reports of famines and disease in various regions

- Earthquakes that reach large readings on the Richter scale

- Churches reporting findings of old religious texts or relics that are improbable, and most likely fraudulent.

- Appearance of individuals that perform miracles, claiming to be performing them due to religious enlightenment.

- Rise in 'alternative' religions such as the Occult and Witchcraft.

- Claims by religious groups that they know where and when Jesus will re-appear.

- Increase in anti-Christian and anti-Semitic activity, either through protests or violence.

- General apathy by world governments in the face of anti-Christian and anti-Semitic material or activity

- Occurrence of unusual planetary alignments and cosmic phenomenon such as eclipses and meteor showers.

- Formation of a global government, either as a consortium of various national countries or a coalition of economic entities led by a charismatic leader that touts ambitious and positive solutions to the ills of the world.

- The policies of the charismatic leader mentioned above change drastically but without opposition after 3 and a half years. The policies become more totalitarian in nature.

- Widespread introduction of RFID (Radio Frequency Identification) or silicon based chips implanted in humans as a new standard for personal financial transactions and identification security.

- The implanted RFID chips work in a broad range of Frequencies (High, Ultra High, Low and Ultra Low) but the final frequency is a constituent or multiple of 666.

Reacting

If all the signs above have occurred then a large number of natural afflictions should begin to occur on the earth. This will include large hail storms, earthquakes, floods and severe and unusual weather. If you are living in an urban area that is relatively close to sea level in height (under 200 yards) or in distance (within 10 miles) then you must evacuate your property. The nature of the cataclysm that will affect earth is widespread and pervasive everywhere so the need for a shelter is obvious, but the location is not particularly specific although urban areas can and should be used.

If you are at a higher altitude or the area you live in is relatively out of reach from coastal areas then you are better off staying put, securing your area and immediately start scouring for supplies.

Surviving

Finding Shelter

Gravitate towards Business Parks and Industrial areas

Once again, business parks and industrial estates are perfect, as they have few residential areas nearby, good transport access as well as offering good prospects for foraging and are usually outside large cities. Most importantly, they are usually religiously neutral.

In a biblical Apocalypse, there will be heavy rioting, looting, as well as spates of hate crime and religiously fuelled violence. To prevent this, curfews or quarantines in any large cities may come into force to stem the violence.

To avoid this, you would need to leave large cities and towns immediately and avoid any religiously ethnic areas as violence would be concentrated in these vicinities. Churches, Mosques and Temples of all denominations should all be avoided as they would be the focus of potentially volatile situations.

Your shelter situation should also be dictated by proximity to the sea. If possible, you must find shelter that is on a relatively high sea level (1 mile+) as well as staying clear of earthquake fault lines. Try to stay away from mountainous areas.

As usual, strike a balance between the location of your shelter and the opportunities for foraging. Water should be more plentiful in this scenario as there will be ample rain, as well as coastal storms. Refer to the chapter on Water on how to purify it, and refer to the chapter on food so you know what to forage for.

Mark of the beast

The Mark of the beast has been a source of much contention for theorists for a long time. Some medieval historians believed the bubonic plague to be the mark of the beast as the disease scoured Europe of life.

It must be noted here that the mark of the beast is a purely Christian theological symbol and does not feature so succinctly in other religions. Religions such as Islam have their own versions of Armageddon but signs of this impending doom are not as clearly distinguished nor as widely known as the Christian version.

There are few options for survival in this scenario. To survive, you must be rid of the mark of the beast, and accept god as your savior so that you won't perish.

Proponents of biblical apocalypse advocate that the mark of the beast is what will identify those that should die. The most obvious solution therefore is to remove it so that its influence on your destiny is removed.

Although doomsday theorists will argue about what exactly constitutes the mark of the beast, it seems the majority agree that the mark is the RFID chip (Radio Frequency Identification). These chips are commonplace today yet most people are not readily aware of their implications. A clever invention, they were initially used as an audit control and logistical aid for companies to quickly assess stock levels of various goods. As technology has progressed, the use of the chips has grown and now they are used for many other applications. Eventually theorists predict they will be implanted under the skin and form part of your identity. They could be used for accessing your bank details or as a biometric passport, all simply accessed through a scanner.

The RFID will be located in either the back of your hand or your forehead, or both. It is about 10mm long and will be buried only a few mm under your skin. The chips can be destroyed by puncturing, crushing or microwaving them but this presents a specific problem if found under the skin. They are waterproof and cannot be demagnetized. They have no battery due to their size but receive their energy from the radio signal when they are queried. They are transponders so transmit their unique identification code as a response to a query.

Certain interpretations of prophecy dictate that the crux and central nervous system of this RFID network will be a super-computer that will be used to establish control over the peoples of the earth. This will be under direct control of the Anti-Christ.

One option is to jam the broadcast from what are effectively radio signals. Tin foil is the best commonly available jamming material available and can be used temporarily to stop radio signals by wrapping it several layers around your hands and forehead.

Destroying or disabling the chip permanently while it is under the skin is only possible with blocker tags or an RFID zapper, both of which will be unavailable at the time. The easiest way is crude but effective, as it guarantees destruction of the chip.

⇒ Take aspirin if possible. This will increase bleeding as well as provide slight pain control. Increased bleeding will help 'flush' the chip from the sub-cutaneous layer.

⇒ Use rubbing alcohol, or any alcoholic beverage with 20%+ concentration to cleanse the back of the hand or the forehead

⇒ Cut using a scalpel or knife to the depth of the RFID chip (0.5-1cm) in an X shape, with the centre of the X landing on the position of the chip

⇒ Let the wound bleed out. If you have taken aspirin it will not clot.

⇒ Using tweezers, a needle or the tip of the knife lever the chip outwards or towards the surface.

⇒ Wash the wound with ample water and bandage the wound

Once you have the physical chip, you can destroy it easily by puncturing it, crushing it or burning it. If your microwave is still functioning, a few seconds will completely overload the circuit and render it useless.

Accepting god as your savior

The only known secure method to avoid Armageddon is accepting god as your savior. This step is very simple and does not necessarily have to be emotional, but spiritual in nature. The physical effects of the Armageddon such as a meteor strike, plague and earthquakes will no doubt instill you with a vigorous and renewed sense of spirituality.

"Everyone who calls on the name of the Lord will be saved." (Romans 10:13)

This means to accept him as your savior you must pray. Prayer is a very individual and personal endeavor. The disciples once asked Jesus: *"Teach us how to pray" (Luke 11,1)*. He ended up teaching them what is now known as the 'Lords Prayer'. The prayer is as follows:

Our Father, who art in heaven,
hallowed be thy name;
thy kingdom come;
thy will be done of earth as it is in heaven.
Give us this day our daily bread;
and forgive us our trespasses
as we forgive those who trespass against us;
and lead us not into temptation
but deliver us from evil

Alternatively, you can say the following prayer to admit your conviction in god. This is a prayer called 'The Apostles Creed'

I believe in God, the Father almighty,
creator of heaven and earth.

I believe in Jesus Christ, God's only Son, our Lord,
who was conceived by the Holy Spirit,
born of the Virgin Mary,
suffered under Pontius Pilate,
was crucified, died, and was buried;
he descended to the dead.
On the third day he rose again;
he ascended into heaven,
he is seated at the right hand of the Father,
and he will come again to judge the living and the dead.

I believe in the Holy Spirit,
the holy catholic church,
the communion of saints,
the forgiveness of sins,
the resurrection of the body,
and the life everlasting.

Once this is done with conviction you have accepted god as your savior and will be spared the fate of the end.

Survivors

Survivors in this scenario refer to those that survive the environmental cataclysms that affect the earth before the second coming. If they have a mark of the beast it is best to actively avoid them, while those that have accepted god as their savior will serve as good company and reassurance in these troubled times. They can be used to increase your knowledge of the bible and you can pray together, and it will be easier for you both to forage supplies as you can cover a greater distance. There is much debate on whether all non-believers will be destroyed at this time, as well as to what extent those with the mark of the beast will survive (if at all!). It is generally accepted though, that survivors will only be those worthy of heavens abode.

Post Apocalypse

The earth after Armageddon, although having being completely destroyed by natural phenomena and war will be rebuilt. Although interpretations differ, those that have the mark of the beast and follow the anti-Christ will cease to exist in the minds of the living and will effectively be purged from the earth. This will leave all those worthy enough to rebuild earth to the paradise it was meant to be and effectively transform it into gods' kingdom. This is said to last 1000 years.

METEORITE

Threat level	Extremely low
Length of Crisis	2-6 weeks
Odds of Survival – prepared	50%
Odds of Survival – unprepared	15%
Foraging opportunities	Poor

Survival kit List

2	1 quart Container of Sterile water	2	Disposable scalpels
30	100mg caffeine tablets	12	Duct Tape
1	5 gallon water container (full)	6	Flares
1	50 Ft Monofilament Line	1	Folding camper's stove
12	Absorbent cotton rags	24	Hexamine blocks
1	Aloe Vera burn ointment	1	Inflatable splints
1	Anti-biotic ointment	1	large bottle 1000mg vitamin C
500	Aspirin	1	Large bottle Multivitamin
12	Assorted Fishhooks	1	Long Tweezers
1	Axe/Hatchet	1	Magnesium bar w/flint insert
1	Bandage scissors	1	Magnifying Glass
2	bandages elastic, self adhesive	30	Meals Ready to eat (24 hour pack)
12	Batteries - various sizes (pack)	1	Multi-sizing wrench
1	Butane lighter	12	N-95/P3 Particulate mask
1	Can opener - Hand operated	2	Nails/screws/bolts - (bag)
1	Claw Hammer	1	Needle and Thread
5	collapsible 5 ga. Water Containers	200	Plastic bin liner
1	condoms (packet of 12)	1	Protective goggles
1	Crowbar/Prying bar	1	Rubbing Alcohol
12	Disposable gloves	1	Signal Mirror

Effects

Cosmic collisions occur on a constant level, whether it is between two small pebbles or two stars. Earth itself frequently collides with particles of different sizes, but these produce no noticeable effect as most objects will burn up in the atmosphere before they ever reach the surface. There are many search projects active for what are referred to as Near Earth Objects (NEO's). These search programs track the size and frequency of asteroids or objects and their proximity to the earth. The frequency of NEO's recorded yearly increased at an almost exponential rate, but this is perhaps due more to an increase in accuracy of the search projects rather than a real increase in the frequency of NEO's. At time of writing, 8000 NEO's have been recorded with a mass width of 1 meter or more in the space of a year. These usually miss the earth by thousands of kilometers but there have been just as many that miss the earth by a few kilometers or enter the atmosphere. Earth is abundant with meteor craters that are a testament to the reality that meteors can and do strike the earth. Many theorists believe that meteors themselves are responsible for various seismic events and the subsequent extinction of many ancient species, notably the dinosaurs, although this still holds much potential for debate.

A definitive earth ending meteorite is possible, but not too probable. For the purposes of survival there is a difference between a meteorite that would destroy all life on the planet compared with a meteorite that would destroy life as we know it. We currently ponder the former.

The effects of this meteorite would be cataclysmic. A meteorite that effectively ends almost all life on earth would be approximately 300 miles in diameter. It would most likely land in the body of water that encompasses 70% of the earth. It would land at a speed ranging from 30-40 miles per second (slightly slower than a comet) and it would most likely impact at an angle of 45 degrees.

On impact it would cause a fireball akin to a nuclear weapon of approximately 2500 megatons. It would open a crater in the water about 3500 miles wide, and even when it gets to the sea floor (for an average depth of 150 feet of water), the crater would be over 1800 miles wide. This would vaporize huge volumes of water and shoot condensed vapor across almost the entire globe. The fireball would expand to as far as 4000 miles wide, setting everything flammable alight as well as causing 3rd degree burns to everyone exposed, if not incinerating them completely. The area would also be irradiated for up to 3 days, making the area unapproachable by anyone. At a distance of even 12,000 miles away the impact would be felt in the form of an earthquake which would arrive just over an hour after impact. This earthquake would register anywhere from 9 to 14 on the Richter scale, which is more powerful than any recorded earthquake in history. Even at this distance, this would damage most legacy structures (churches, etc.) but most modern buildings should only suffer minor damage. 16 hours after the effects of the earthquake the air blast will arrive, and again at a distance of 12,000 miles (basically the furthest possible point from the impact) there will be significant damage. The blast will first of all burst the ear drums of everyone at this distance. It will also cause multi-storey buildings to collapse, unless they are steel framed and even then they will suffer extreme distortion. Bridges will shatter and collapse, regardless of whether they are suspended or what materials they were built with. All stationary vehicles will be flung dozens of meters and suffer severe damage. Almost all trees will be uprooted, and the remainder stripped of all leaves and fruit. Although people are reasonably resistant to changes in air pressure, the sheer violence and speed of this air blast will cause major trauma and fractures by flinging people literally hundreds of meters as well as being subject to shrapnel and debris traveling through the air at ballistic speeds. Any human caught outside at the time of the air blast has virtually no chance of survival.

Below is a diagram on the effects of the impact, assuming a meteor of approximately 500km in diameter.

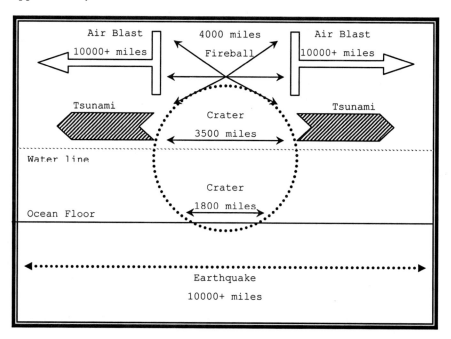

Detecting

- Reports from NEO projects that a large previously unidentified meteor is on a collision course with earth.

- Comet does not show up on previous NEO tracking charts and causes widespread alarm.

- Sudden disruption of all satellite based communication systems on a global scale.

- Reports of unscheduled lunar or solar eclipses or other cosmic phenomenon attributed to the above warnings

- Reports of Bluish columns of light moving across the sky in a column or streak.

- Air raid sirens or emergency broadcasts in conjunction with the above warnings

Reacting

The reaction to the meteorite is based on the assumption that you are 9,000-12,000 miles away from the point of impact. In general terms this means the opposite hemisphere to the impact, as most of the opposing side of the earth will feel effects too severe to make survival possible.

As soon you learn a meteorite impact is imminent, you must act quickly. You have time allotted to you on the basis of how far away the meteorite is from impact. The first effect that will reach you is the earthquake, which will arrive within 45 minutes to an hour and a half. The earthquake will damage most structures, especially if they are old. Steel reinforced buildings, such as modern office buildings will survive easily.

Basics of Earthquake survival are as follows:

⇒ Do not panic and run. The ground will feel unstable but it is rare for it to tear open and swallow you up. A lot of the injury caused in earthquakes comes from debris and shrapnel and the collapse of poorly built structures.

⇒ If you are inside get under a desk, table, doorway or kneel next to an inside wall and secure yourself. Make sure you have positioned yourself away from windows, mirrors and shelves and cover your face to protect it from shattering glass.

⇒ If you are outside stay away from loose or poorly built structures or structure that are made of wood. Distance yourself from large trees, telephone and electrical wires. Sit or lie down as the earth will be extremely unsteady. Cover your head to protect yourself from small debris.

⇒ If you are driving, stay away from bridges, utility poles and trees and try to park your car in flat open areas. There is no need to leave your vehicle as it will provide you some degree of protection against falling objects.

Once the shaking has ceased you must wait a few minutes so that all debris and loose objects have had time to fall. There will be the potential for after-shocks that won't be as severe but the above precautions can be repeated if necessary.

After the earthquake has subsided you will have approximately 14-16 hours before the arrival of the most serious threat in this scenario: the air blast.

The only way to survive the air blast is to find suitable cover, so this will involve going back inside. Most individuals who survive the earthquake will instinctively move outside to survey the damage. The shelters that will offer the best degree of protection against the air blast will be conventional bomb and tornado shelters. Basement shelters will also be useful, especially if they are situated in steel framed buildings.

Most people have no access to professional shelters, so an improvised shelter will have to be used. Basement shelters can be found anywhere in an urban environment. Wine cellars, larders and refuse rooms make ideal improvised shelters. Staying in a city is not recommended as the air blast will instigate the collapse of most buildings, even steel framed ones which will produce too much rubble to make an exit from the basement possible after the air blast has passed.

The ideal scenario then is finding the nearest small town or rural area that is above sea level and away from urban areas. If a makeshift shelter can be found in a property, then use it. Ideally it should not be near any other large buildings. Any supplies that you intend on keeping should be gathered now as anything left above ground will be blown away. Use the Chapter on food to make a list of the best items to gather, and make sure you have as much bottled water as will fit into the shelter. Time your foraging trips to two hours only, leaving plenty of time to return to your shelter, unload your provisions and take cover.

Lie on the floor face down and cover yourself with a blanket or coat or whatever material you can. Lie with your head away from the exit while covering your ears at the same time.

When the blast comes it will no doubt destroy the structure above the basement and blow it away. The trapdoor or access door to the cellar may be ripped from its hinges and blown away. This will fill the cellar with dust and debris as well and you will feel a strong updraft.

The air blast will pass extremely quickly. Once it is over, stay in position for several minutes until the dust has settled in your shelter. This will also allow any swirling debris outside to fall and settle, preventing further injury.

Surviving

Once you have survived the initial blast and its after-effects, the main threat is over. Your survival routine going forward should consist of the following activities, prioritized in this order:

- Foraging for food, water and supplies

- Constructing a new shelter away from previous urban environments

- Erecting banners and signals to attract survivors

Be warned that there will be 'aftershocks' as the earth stabilizes and tectonic plates will not have settled due to the intensity of the impact. You should also try and cover your mouth and eyes where possible to avoid becoming exposed to toxic particles. The impact will no doubt produce fallout in many forms, and this will mainly be in the form of heavy metal particles or other toxic substances that will be produced by wholesale destruction of urban areas. It is unlikely that these particles are radioactive but they will cause damage to your lungs if they are inhaled. Fallout may persist depending on prevailing weather conditions but within two weeks most fallout will have receded to acceptable levels. You should however, after this time still cover your mouth with whatever protection you have as there will be persisting fires from destroyed urban areas and vehicles.

In the weeks following the impact you'll observe many turbulent and atypical weather phenomena that aren't seasonally related. This could be anything from violent storms to thick fog. It will last several weeks after which it will return to the normal pre-impact weather cycle. This turbulent weather will hasten the need for an adequate shelter to prevent your exposure to the elements. There will be few structures remaining in an urban area. Those that have survived (mostly steel framed buildings) will have suffered core damage due to the earthquake and subsequent air blast in addition to damage from nearby buildings of lesser stature falling or collapsing around them.

Although it is more labor intensive, a shelter will have to be constructed as there will be few dependable structures remaining. For the first few weeks following the impact, the type of shelter constructed will have to be as temporary as possible. This is due to the potential for aftershocks in the wake of the impact. Aftershocks will hinder your construction efforts and may put an end to your shelter prematurely if you endeavor to build a more permanent home.

For this reason, construct something temporary but effective. The simplest shelter to construct in terms of labor and materials is earth based fallout shelter. Although traditionally used to protect from the effects of nuclear fallout and its associated hazards, it will also benefit survivors of the meteor impact a great deal. View the 'Nuclear' chapter to view the diagram of the shelter.

After several weeks have passed, you can move to construct a more permanent shelter or seek out another location which may have surviving structures. What you build will depend entirely on your skills, ingenuity as well as the materials available. Destroyed urban areas will provide an abundant source for building materials and will be a good place to start. You can remain in your fallout shelter, expanding and improving it as necessary or you can move above ground, inhabiting old structures which you improve with whatever new materials you have or merely creating something simple such as a tent house protected by tarpaulin and sheeting. Try to stay away from areas which have suffered erosion caused by earthquake damage as well as low lying river or swamp areas to prevent flooding.

Survivors

Treatment of survivors in this scenario should be as friends. There is no benefit to excluding survivors unless they are severely delusional or too injured to be of any assistance. Foraging in collapsed urban structures will require additional aid in the form of light and transport assistance, all of which will be difficult to accomplish alone. Survivor numbers should be small at first, perhaps less than a dozen people, but over time will increase as they come into contact with other such survivor communities. Damage caused by the meteor impact will leave a harsh desolate world which will be difficult to survive in alone so forming groups will benefit everyone.

The only threat in this instance is the presence of survivor communities with cannibalistic tendencies which may appear in areas that have been hit particularly hard by the meteor and that offer no foraging opportunities. These communities will have a very vicious tribal nature led by one totalitarian leader. Such survivor communities should be avoided or if possible, destroyed.

Post Apocalypse

A Meteor apocalypse leaves a hideously disfigured world. Where there once were oceans, there are now barren craters devoid of all life. Where there was once a city, there is now a sea. A world ending meteor may also produce a very slight effect on the tilt and rotation of the earth. Although this may not have any obvious effect initially, later this will produce variations in the length and temperature of seasons. It may also cause days to be longer or shorter in regards to daylight at various times of the year.

On the safest side of the earth it leaves a terrain not directly affected by the meteor strike but having taken the brunt of ferocious seismic activity and a crippling blast wave. Most of the land will be littered with ruins. Plants and crops will have been ripped from the earth by the roots and flung far and wide. This will produce an interesting ecosystem as over time, this dispersal of seeds would create diverse and new vegetation colonies on top of and around former urban areas and would attract wide ranging fauna. Long term Survival in this environment would be affected only by the availability of food. Foraging canned goods from former urban areas would last anywhere from 2-4 years depending on how far you scavenge. After this, you would resort to an agrarian lifestyle which would be well supported by the new availability of plant life.

ALIENS

Threat level	Low
Length of Crisis	6-18 months
Odds of Survival – prepared	75%
Odds of Survival – unprepared	25%
Foraging opportunities	Moderate

Survival kit List

1	.22 caliber pistol	1	condoms (packet of 12)
500	.22 caliber pistol ammunition	1	Crowbar/Prying bar
2	1 quart Container of Sterile water	12	Disposable gloves
30	100mg caffeine tablets	2	Disposable scalpels
2	5 Gallon water container (full)	12	Duct Tape
1	50 Ft Monofilament Line	6	Flares
12	Absorbent cotton rags	1	Folding camper's stove
1	Aloe Vera burn ointment	24	Hexamine blocks
1	Anti-biotic ointment	1	large bottle 1000mg chewable Vitai
500	Aspirin	1	Large bottle Multivitamin
12	Assorted Fishhooks	1	Long Tweezers
1	Axe/Hatchet	1	Magnesium bar w/flint insert
1	Bandage scissors	1	Magnifying Glass
2	bandages elastic, self adhesive	30	Meals Ready to eat (24 hour pack)
12	Batteries - various sizes (pack)	1	Multi-band Receiver/Scanner
1	Bowie Knife	1	Multi-sizing wrench
1	Butane lighter	2	Nails/screws/bolts - various sizes (
1	Can opener - Hand operated	1	Needle and Thread
1	Claw Hammer	200	Plastic bin liner
5	Collapsible 5 ga. Containers	1	Rubbing Alcohol

Effects

Alien invasion is something which we disregard but if ever faced with it, it would produce very sudden and long lasting effects. Alien invasion in this context refers to extra-terrestrial life forms overtly arriving to take ownership of the planet. The effects following describe the most probable overt invasion scenario, although no one can effectively predict the outcome of one.

Current information on alien life forms is sparse, vague and unconfirmed. There are many theories on the potential route for invasion an alien force would take if this did occur. These range from an attack by organic spores to aliens that effectively clone and replace humans one by one. However, the most popular theory suited to apocalyptic levels of destruction is an invasion by a military inclined force bent on the destruction of the human race and occupation of the entire earth.

Arrival of these aliens would most likely occur in or just outside dense urban areas. This arrival would be nearly simultaneous in all parts of the globe, or would arrive in sequence from one hemisphere to another. A reconnaissance party of anywhere up to a dozen craft would arrive for scouting and clearing duties, clearing the way for the larger fleet to install itself at the landing site.

The offensive vessels of the alien invasion would either be contained within the alien craft, or would be the craft themselves. For the purposes of destruction, the alien arsenal would consist of mostly tactical weapons as large scale annihilation of the earth would scupper the main purpose of the alien invasion, most likely to be cultivation of the planets natural resources.

Their weapons would be either neutron based which would severely affect humans while leaving buildings and other structures standing or would be based on thermal radiation and would effectively have a more physical effect on structure and vehicles, setting them alight or disintegrating them altogether. They may also utilize tactical nuclear devices, again likely to be neutron based so that the physically destructive effect is avoided.

The first week of their appearance will result in the large scale destruction of cities, killing up to 75% of city based populations. The simultaneous scale and severity of this destruction will hinder military forces from mounting an effective counter-attack. Once the alien forces have destroyed main cities they will transform these into their communication and logistical hubs to expand outwards to the next largest urban area, repeating the process again. Throughout this time, any human individuals encountered are likely to be destroyed or captured for further study.

In the second week, the first large scale military confrontation with the alien force will occur, ending with a quick defeat and high casualty rates for the human forces. Conventional weapons will prove to have minimal effect, and the alien force will take little, if any casualties. The 3rd week will replicate the pattern of the previous weeks as alien forces spread out even further and encounter less structured resistance. In the fourth week, another military encounter will occur with the remaining human forces, which will be using experimental or unorthodox tactics (including tactical nuclear weapons). These tactics will have some success, inflicting casualties on the alien forces, as well as exposing weaknesses but will also result in high casualty rates for the human military. This is effectively the last co-coordinated overt confrontation that will face the aliens as the command and control and logistical centers of the human military will be too affected and sparse to continue a coherent campaign. After 1 month, alien confrontation with humans will be reduced to cut-off units offering sporadic resistance without any support. All main human population centers will have been wiped out, leaving only very small rural towns or inaccessible villages functioning.

Detecting

- Increased sighting of Unidentified flying objects (UFO's)

- Reports from SETI (Search for Extra-Terrestrial Intelligence) institute of alien signals originating from an unknown source.

- Reports of satellite interference not related to other cosmic phenomenon

- Cosmic phenomenon visible during daylight hours.

- Broadcasts of craters caused by small scale meteor showers on an international scale.

- Reports of simultaneous landings on an international scale of UFO's

- Loss of commercial radio broadcasts and signals after reports of UFO landings

- Large scale military and police convoys moving towards urban areas

- Activation of air raid warning systems, including air raid sirens.

- Emergency broadcast systems activated and deployed, reporting large scale invasion

- Visible alien spacecraft attacking urban areas

Reacting

As soon as the threat of aliens has been confirmed, the first step is to evacuate with haste any and all urban areas by whatever means possible. If stuck in an urban area that is undergoing major destruction by alien forces, you must head into a subway or underground transport system (if available) or head into the nearest makeshift basement. Refuse rooms in office buildings, larders in restaurants or wine cellars all make ideal makeshift basements. If you are stuck in one of these basements, you must wait until the offensive has passed and then leave the urban area.

Once outside you must seek shelter in rural areas. These areas will provide plenty of cover in the form of foliage, as well as unobstructed view on incoming craft. Rural areas will also provide you with access to crop fields and its irrigation systems (for an abundance of water). If available, relegate yourself to higher altitude areas that are mountainous. This will give further access to natural shelter in the form of caves and grottos and be a natural focal point for survivors to gather. Try to avoid traveling in groups as this will attract undue attention. If you have transport make sure it can travel at speed and can navigate off-road terrain.

Surviving

Survival in this scenario depends on how fast and how many survivors can be banded together. In its simplest form, the survival strategy against an alien invasion is to form a cohesive underground movement and adopt guerilla tactics to destroy the alien visitors.

To mount an effective insurgency against the alien invasion the following principles must be followed:

❖ Supplies – Supplies as often as possible must be captured from the alien forces. This reduces the burden on typical foraging for weapons and transport and will hamper the alien force.

❖ Targets – Will always be softer peripheral targets such as communications, logistics and transport elements of the alien force. Only individual military assets should be targeted.

❖ Safe houses – Shelter should be organized ahead of time for guerillas returning from ambush duties or other human elements escaping alien pursuers. These will also act as rendezvous points and secondary headquarters

❖ Intelligence – Squad sized reconnaissance units should be dedicated to gathering intelligence which will assist in the overall insurgency effort. Intelligence should focus on movement of alien forces as well as alien installations and their locations. There is a small chance that aliens may utilize a captive human population for manual labor or other servitude, and a large portion of the Intelligence will focus on gathering inside knowledge and weaknesses of the alien occupier.

❖ Prisoners – A high priority should be capturing alien craft and life forms. This will enable analysis of their weaknesses and the subsequent exploitation of these weaknesses for tactical and strategic advantage.

❖ Hit and Run – The mainstay of the tactics should always be the destruction of alien assets followed by a quick escape. A high rhythm of guerilla attacks will bog down large tracts of alien forces when only a small band of guerillas is being used.

Ambush

A human insurgency will never be able to mount a conventional attack on alien forces once they are established. By utilizing the principles above to harass the occupying forces, the human insurgency will most likely rely on ambush as the main form of attack. Performing a successful ambush will rely on two factors:

1. Placing the ambush site at a natural chokepoint

2. Positioning of insurgents to create maximum kill zone

Ambushes should be setup along regular patrol or supply routes that the alien forces utilize. The ambush itself should never be sprung until the rear of the supply column is in plain sight. Over time, if supply routes are hit often enough, an armed reconnaissance element will be added to scout appropriate routes. This can be easily circumvented by either setting up ambush right after the reconnaissance unit has passed ahead of the column, or camouflaging the ambush positions ahead of time sufficiently enough to prevent discovery.

The diagram below illustrates a basic ambush position.

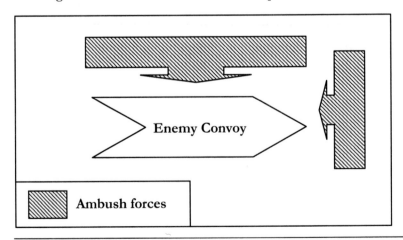

Enemy Convoy

Ambush forces

The aim of an ambush is to inflict the maximum amount of casualties, and not to destroy and entire convoy or enemy force. For this reason, after an initial engagement of approximately 5 minutes, the ambushing forces will withdraw to setup another ambush at a later date. If the ambush is so successful that the convoy is almost wiped out, it is best to finish the job to allow for the capture of alien life forms as well as supplies.

The tempo of ambush attacks should be high, regardless of the damage they inflict. They should also not be confined to a geographic area, and should be carried out on the entire breadth and width of the alien occupation zone.

If a consistent rhythm of attacks carries on, occupying forces will begin to withdraw from areas which have seen significant casualties and a high rate of attacks despite increased security measures. Once the occupying force changes its behavior from pro-active search and destroy to a defensive posture, the tactics utilized must shift from ambush and guerilla attacks to overt and occasional conventional warfare. These engagements must be in areas where humans have superior forces and firepower and utilize the element of surprise. This pattern must continue until all occupying forces are destroyed, or they leave entirely.

Finding weakness

If an alien life form is captured alive, then it must be used to test for weaknesses. The exploitation of weaknesses will offer far more of an advantage to human survivors than a conventional military approach. When testing your live alien prisoner, it will be beneficial to treat it humanely in between treatment sessions. This is to enable the correct detection of weaknesses in good health as opposed to the prisoner reacting adversely to certain stimuli due to exhaustion rather than a genuine weakness or allergy.

Testing a prisoner for weakness is done once the alien is strapped down and secured. Each testing session should be no more than one hour long and there should be no more than 4 such sessions a day.

Finding a weakness without proper facilities will be difficult and will have to be done in more general terms. The alien life form should be exposed to the following and any adverse reactions should be observed:

- Sound: Different levels of volume as well as different frequencies.

- Light: Different intensities as well as the use of different color filters to ascertain weaknesses. If possible, and if available the use of infra-red or ultra-violet rays should be used and any adverse reactions observed.

- Liquids and solvents: Although unlikely, the life form may be sensitive or allergic to various liquids and solvents. The most common solvent to start with is of course water. You can submerge limbs or other parts of the life form for a certain time and observe reactions or see if it reacts negatively to water splashed on its main senses (eyes, ears, etc.)

- Infection: Cut a small wound into a non-vital limb of the alien life form and observe the rate of infection or how quickly it heals. At this stage you can take blood samples and also observe its properties and how it reacts to all the above.

- Vital organs and pressure points: Finally, you will test vital organs of the alien life form by penetrating key locations on its body. Begin with limbs and the body and finish with the head. This will obviously kill the alien but will give an opportunity to detect vital points. Like most life forms, the cerebral cortex will provide the greatest weakness but due to the extra-terrestrial morphology of the alien life form it may end up having vital organs anywhere. Be sure to dissect the dead life form to examine organ location.

Once you have completed all the above tests you can use the results to adapt your tactics. This may include changing the time of day of attacks (if a sensitivity to light occurs) or attacking with certain weapons more than others as well as exploiting vital organs and pressure points to produce more effective ambushes.

Survivors

The availability of survivors will be the difference between success and failure in this scenario. Due to the nature of the cataclysm, it is unlikely that surviving communities differ in purpose save for eliminating the alien occupation. All survivors should be utilized to their fullest, including the young and elderly which can be used for back end logistical assistance (i.e. Foraging) or non-combative duties (reconnaissance). Surviving military units will be premium as they will bring trained personnel as well as remaining military hardware. There is little, if any, chance of meeting hostile survivors in this scenario apart from those that have been living under alien occupation that are perhaps brainwashed or others which are so psychologically damaged that they are aggressive to all strangers.

Post-Apocalypse

Alien invasion will leave a hybridized world now devoid of human urban existence but abundant with alien artifacts once the alien invasion has been repulsed (if indeed this is the case). This will serve a dual purpose in both speeding up the recovery of civilization to the pre-apocalyptic level of technology as well as in certain cases advancing technology beyond the knowledge of human endeavor. Prognosis for human survival in this instance is good, due to the abundant access to Alien technology that it will leave for surviving communities.

ZOMBIES

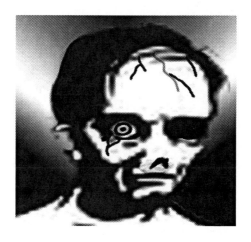

Threat level	Extremely low
Length of Crisis	6-18 months
Odds of Survival – prepared	85%
Odds of Survival – unprepared	40%
Foraging opportunities	Good

Survival kit List

1	.22 caliber pistol	1	Condoms (packet of 12)
500	.22 caliber pistol ammunition	1	Cotton balls (packet of 200)
2	1 quart Container of Sterile water	1	Crowbar/Prying bar
2	5 gallon water container (full)	12	Disposable gloves
30	100mg caffeine tablets	2	Disposable scalpels
1	50 Ft Monofilament Line	12	Duct Tape
12	Batteries – various sizes (packet)	6	Flares
12	Absorbent cotton rags	1	Folding camper's stove
1	Aloe Vera burn ointment	24	Hexamine blocks
1	Anti-biotic ointment	1	Lge bottle 1000mg vitamin C
500	Aspirin	1	Lge bottle Multivitamins
12	Assorted Fishhooks	1	Long Tweezers
1	Axe/Hatchet	1	Magnesium bar w/flint insert
1	Bandage scissors	1	Magnifying Glass
2	Bandages elastic, self adhesive	30	Meals Ready to eat (24 hour pack)
1	Bowie Knife	1	Multi-band Receiver/Scanner
1	Butane lighter	1	Multi-sizing wrench
1	Can opener - Hand operated	2	Nails/screws/bolts - (bag)
1	Claw Hammer	1	Needle and Thread
5	Collapsible 5 gal.water containers	200	Plastic bin liner

Effects

Zombies. Re-animated corpses. The Undead. A pandemic that is both frightening in speed and complexity.

The causes of the zombification are unknown but theorists believe it can stem from excessive radiation exposure, contact with an alien organism or merely the result of an infectious disease.

The Epidemiology of the affliction is similar in scope to direct contact transmission infections. The host will transmit the pathogen through direct and usually aggressive contact. Bites, abrasions and punctured skin all provide a potent vehicle for the transmission of the effect. In addition to this, secondary infections can occur due to the necrotic flesh of the host body which can develop into a myriad of bacterial infections such as Sepsis.

Once infected, a person will start to exhibit symptoms of fever, heart palpitations as well as clammy skin. Depending on the severity of the infection, the individual will suffer from increased fever, nausea and dizziness until they lapse into unconsciousness, quickly followed by death. Death can occur anywhere between a day to a week of initial infection depending on the severity of the infection. Re-animation of the cadaver occurs within 2-4 minutes of death. This means the cadaver will rise from where it died and begin exploring and seeking further victims. All former traces of the human host including personality, language and fine motor functions will have been lost.

There is no treatment to halt the spread of infection, save for immediate dismemberment of affected limbs or digits and cauterizing the resulting wound. If the wound is located elsewhere, there is little chance for survival.

Once re-animated the movement, motor-functions and behavior of the recently deceased can vary wildly. Movement can be catatonic and irregular or purposeful and driven. Motor-functions of zombies can be clumsy and awkward and may or may not improve throughout the life cycle of the infection.

Hosts will exhibit aggression, and this is ultimately what drives the diffusion of infection within a population and is perhaps the self-preservation mechanism of the virus. Size, gender, age and former personality traits have no bearing on the level or consistency of aggression. This is the main catalyst for the spread of infection and this behavior continues until the host is destroyed.

Re-animated bodies have the auditory and sensory capabilities which match the state of the cadaver that hosts the infection and can react to a combination of heat, light, sound or visual cues.

The bodies themselves, effectively housed in necrotic flesh have no reactions to pain or sensory stimuli of any kind. This includes perforations of their outer membrane, destruction of muscle or connective tissue and even amputation of limbs and digits. The afflicted entities do not exhibit fear, nor any emotional responses save for a primal aggression based solely on the carrier to spread.

Movement and function cease when the cerebral cortex is destroyed or when the body of the host is so badly damaged it cannot sustain mobility any further.

The spread of infection is rapid and unforgiving. Due to the nature of the affliction, it is impossible to treat medically and difficult to contain physically. The aggressive and mobile hosts attack every individual within sight and continue to do so regardless of their success rate. Although not physically overpowering, the relentless nature of the mobile cadavers and the difficulty in destroying them, not to mention the psychological trauma of having to face a re-animated corpse frequently results in injury when engaged in melee.

The spread of the Zombie affliction will follow the pattern of expansion diffusion as an increasing number of the local populace are attacked, and through relocation diffusion, when recently infected (alive) individuals are fleeing the area to nearby population centers. Below is a diagram illustrating the basic spread of the affliction.

Diagram of infection spread pattern

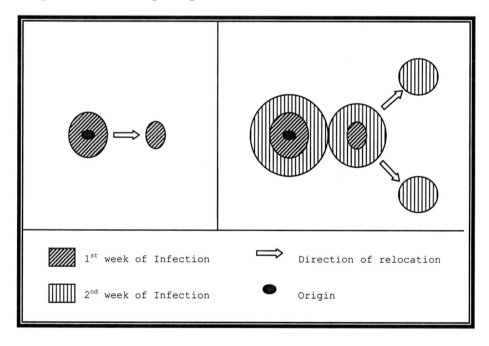

▨	1st week of Infection	⇨	Direction of relocation
▥	2nd week of Infection	●	Origin

Detecting

The first step in surviving a Zombie pandemic is being aware of the warning signs so that you can plan your survival and react effectively.

The following are symptomatic of an impending Zombie Apocalypse:

- Higher than usual incidence of violence or rioting in the immediate area that has no particular source or obvious cause.

- Unusual or incoherent media broadcasts about an upsurge in violence which has no demographic pattern (racial or otherwise).

- Reports of unusual demeanor on the part of perpetrators of the violence, citing psychosis or hyper-aggression.

- Reports of large numbers of mutilated or cannibalized corpses found within an urban area.

- Emergency Medical Services reporting increased numbers of casualties suffering from biting and claw wounds.

- Changes in the threat level or announcements of city wide curfews or terrorist alerts in relation to the above disturbances.

- Sightings of re-animated corpses or talk of attacked victims succumbing to their wounds and returning to life.

- Quarantine announcements of particular buildings, sites or districts within an urbanized area, especially when in conjunction with the above occurrences.

- Large scale military influx of personnel and vehicles within an urbanized area.

- An increase in frequency and severity of the above occurrences as well as similar reports emanating from nearby population centers.

Reacting

Once a pandemic is upon you, the prime focus has to be for you to extricate yourself from any urban areas or areas of high population density. This effectively excludes going near any town or city with a substantial pre-pandemic population if you are to establish an effective survival strategy. Any large population centre will provide many complications that previously would benefit a pre-pandemic society but due to the nature of the affliction these should be avoided where possible.

Pre-Pandemic City	Pandemic City
• Readily available access to medical and police services	• Services and Infrastructure crippled by increased demand.
• Many available options for transport around urban areas	• Quarantine and curfews restrict transport and mobility.
• Many commercial sources for fuels, food and supplies	• Quarantine and looting disrupt available supplies and produce shortages.
• Large population provides active social life and cultural diversity as well as economic benefits.	• Large population provides increased chance of infection and faster spread of pandemic.

Surviving

Finding Shelter

In the event of a zombie pandemic, finding a suitable shelter is the basis of your long term survival. Stick to the following guidelines:

Stay away from cities

This cannot be stressed enough. Former high density areas will have suffered a higher rate of infection which in turn will have produced a large number of ambulatory corpses.

Opportunities for finding supplies in urban areas are poor. Cities are not storage hubs for any kind of supplies due to the premium placed on storage space. Perishable foods will be commonplace in any household or flat as well as most business premises in a city but their quality degrades over time. Add to this a lack of refrigeration or sanitation and you can safely discount a city for finding sustainable supplies.

Roads in cities will typically be blocked due to previous quarantine measures, abandoned or crashed vehicles and debris caused by looting and/or zombie related damage. This makes transportation around a city difficult unless you are on foot or bike.

Gravitate towards Business Parks and Industrial areas

Business Parks and Industrial areas are typically situated outside cities or large residential areas. They are commercial in nature only and have little, if any residential capacity. Structures such as shopping malls, warehouses or manufacturing facilities are all found in such areas. For this very reason they will be ideal for your survival. Usually situated near major transport arteries they provide good transportation routes into and out of the shelter. A low pre-pandemic population will significantly reduce the danger posed by zombies and roaming undead. In addition to this, large commercial areas will provide an abundance of supplies which will assist you in your survival.

Secure your residence

Once you have found a suitable location, you must secure it. Start with an inspection of the areas surrounding the building/structure that you will reside in. If the area has a fence, walk along the perimeter and note any damage, holes or gaps in the fence. These must be dealt with first. The area around your residence should ideally have two entry and exit points that are accessible by vehicle and at least one auxiliary point that can be accessed on foot in case of an emergency.

Access points on the perimeter should be secured with a gate or other barrier. You can use a second vehicle, crates, barrels, or any debris. It is imperative that this access point can be opened as quickly as it can be closed and if possible from a position which doesn't entail leaving your vehicle when you enter or leave the property.

If there is no obvious perimeter, or the former perimeter is too badly damaged, then one will have to be created at a later date. If you have just arrived, then the safety and security of the main property should have priority over creating a new perimeter.

Security is always established from the ground up and from the outside to the inside. With this in mind, walk the circumference of your property checking and noting windows, ventilation shafts, service entrances and emergency entrances. Replicating what you did for your perimeter, leave two access points and one emergency exit point. All windows on lower floors that do not have safety grills must be boarded over. Use wood, sheeting or even cardboard to secure these. This is to stop visibility into the property, and to insulate it so that light and sound does not escape easily. It will also protect the windows from being shattered and providing unwelcome guests into your abode. Once your access points are established, paint or board over all other access points. Do not block or board over ventilation shafts, unless they provide an obvious access point.

Foraging

Once you have established your shelter, you must busy yourself with surviving. Surviving in the event of a Zombie apocalypse is based around outlasting the undead hordes as zombies are in essence putrefying flesh that have a limited life cycle. Decay will eventually overtake even the most resilient undead corpse and render it immobile given the time and exposure to the elements.

The ease with which you can survive will depend on:

⇒ The amount of food, water and supplies you have access to

⇒ The security and integrity of your shelter

⇒ The number of zombies in the immediate vicinity

Once you have secured your shelter and determined entry and exit points then you must begin foraging for supplies immediately. The sooner you begin gathering supplies the less danger zombies will pose, as they will still be localized in and around urban centers. Zombie numbers will eventually diffuse and spread to the surrounding unpopulated areas naturally, as well as being distracted or drawn by noise, light and heat either natural or man-made.

Every time you are out foraging, if you are in a vehicle make sure you refuel as soon as possible. Siphon fuel from abandoned cars and always get more than you need. Fuel has many uses and can be used for refueling a vehicle, heating, cooking and even for zombie deterrence. After you have collected fuel the onus should then be on water, food, medical and hygiene supplies, construction materials and weapons, in that order. Only make one trip a day, but make sure you fully load your vehicle. If your vehicle has insufficient storage space, then collect only one category of supplies every day. As far as your clothing is concerned, dress yourself in anything protective. Most likely, leather jackets, gloves and trousers will provide a good natural defense and be readily available. If you are fortunate enough to find surplus stores then opt for anything which is 'stab-resistant' as this will no doubt contain Kevlar, a highly resistant material used in the production of anti-ballistic and anti-stab vests. Kevlar will prove a great asset against any bites or scratches, if you manage to find some.

Alternate your scavenging to a different location every day if possible so that chances for finding what you need are maximized. As time progresses, you want to reduce your outings until you are foraging in the immediate surroundings of your shelter. If you are lucky you will continually be able to make long range scavenging excursions for as long as you need, but this will depend entirely on your supplies of fuel, and if there is an increasing concentration of zombies in the vicinity that you scavenge.

Below is a diagram of a foraging pattern you can follow in this scenario.

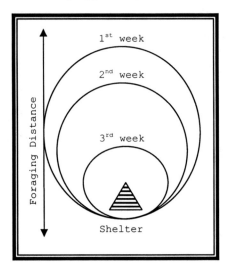

Make lists of what you need before you go out scavenging. Refer to the food and water chapters to see how much you need and plan accordingly. Medical and hygiene supplies will not require the same amount of restocking as food and water, nor will construction materials or weapons (unless you require ammunition for firearms). To survive you will need at most between 6 months to 1 year of supplies of all kinds. Within a year, most zombies will be reduced to rotting puddles of flesh or be so decayed that they pose no threat at all. The rate of decay will depend on many factors such as the initial condition of the zombies when they were infected, the amount of time they have been exposed to the elements, and the amount of activity they have sustained in their infected state.

Defending yourself

Your greatest foe in this apocalypse will be the undead. Knowing your enemy and being able to defend yourself will increase your chances of survival. While on foraging expeditions you will probably be exposed to them a great deal. Observe whether they shamble or run towards you. Do they detect you visually, or are they reacting to sound, light or other stimuli. Are their reactions sharp and responsive or delayed and lethargic? Whatever the variation of zombie you are dealing with they will always share common weaknesses: The cerebral cortex. By destroying the brain or severely damaging it, they will be rendered harmless and pose no further threat. Furthermore, destroying one or both knees will severely reduce their mobility and threat. Zombies will still drag themselves forward using their arms (if they still have them) but destroying their capacity for motion by destroying a leg is easier and less dangerous than attacking the head. On the following pages you will find various tactics for dealing with them should you be unfortunate enough to find yourself face to face with one or more undead.

Confrontation with a single undead

Below is a diagram showing how you should attack a zombie in a one on one situation. The weak areas of the zombie are pointed out for you. Bludgeoning weapons will work best as even a relatively small person can exert enough power to bring down a Zombie provided they hit the right area. Cutting or stabbing weapons will not be as effective as they will not provide enough force to damage the joints or cerebral cortex through the necrotic flesh of the ambulatory corpse.

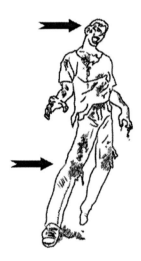

Confrontation with multiple undead

Zombies when alone pose no significant threat and can be easily dispatched provided their weaknesses are exploited and you have the right weapon. When confronted with two or more zombies your advantage will come from your ability to reposition yourself quickly so that one of the zombies creates a natural barrier for the other.

Use your movement to align yourself with a zombie to prevent the others reaching you. Then dispatch the lead zombie in the same manner you would use in a one-on-one situation before moving on to engage his companions.

Diagram 1 – Confrontation with multiple undead

As you can see above this position is not desirable as you are exposed on both sides. Any attack on one of the zombies will cause you to overreach and be within range for either zombie to counter-attack. It is a priority for you to move out of this position to either side of the zombies so that one of them creates a natural barrier for the other and leaves you in an ideal position to attack the weak points on the corpse.

Diagram 2 – Confrontation with multiple undead

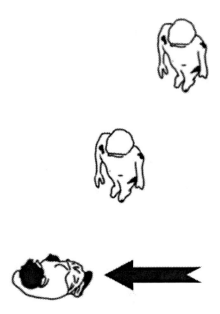

After you have sidestepped you should find yourself in the position above, at which time you can attack the lead zombie in the weak areas pointed out earlier. Once it is dispatched attack the one behind it. Never should you attempt to take on more than two or three zombies in this manner, as any number higher than this will severely affect your ability to weave out of the way and reposition yourself effectively.

The average person has little experience in hand to hand combat and should best avoid combat with undead unless absolutely necessary. This will most often occur during foraging trips, and entering and leaving your residence, especially if a large number of zombies have congested your access points.

Vehicles make a great anti-Zombie weapon if they have built up enough momentum. If you decide to eradicate zombies on a daily basis, make sure you have two separate vehicles, one for your foraging and general utility and another for destroying zombies. You should only use your foraging vehicle for ramming zombies when you need to exit or enter congested areas that have valuable supplies.

Survivors

Survivors in this type of apocalypse are generally welcomed. When you encounter a survivor, unless they are suffering from chills and nausea (typical symptoms of infection) then you join forces if that is their disposition. Infected persons can still be utilized as they may not be aware of their impending fate and should be used while they can, under supervision. You can use infected persons as bait to distract hordes of undead if you need access to a specific area but cannot get in, or as bait in an escape and evasion situation. Elderly survivors, although rare will perhaps hinder you more than aid you. Young children are a boon to survival as they can access crawlspaces and areas that adults otherwise could not. They are also very agile and so more likely to be able to evade Zombies. The advantage of this kind of apocalypse is that survivors will more often than not be specifically skilled or just generally astute in the art of survival. It is your survival, so do not be afraid to sacrifice others for your livelihood. The elderly, children, infected persons or domineering and aggressive survivors can all be used as bait to plan your escape.

Post Apocalypse

When you have reached 6 months you will begin to notice that the threat from Zombies begins to dissipate as they decompose to nothing. Some Zombies may decompose slower than others depending on the weather they've been exposed to and the activity they've sustained. In colder climates some Zombies may persist longer than usual as extreme cold prevents the bacteria necessary for decomposition from forming.

The aftermath of a Zombie Apocalypse will usually leave a healthy abundant environment to sustain agrarian living. Urban areas will suffer mixed fates, as some will have been completely destroyed by the calamity and be awash with wreckage and decay while others may have been quarantined early and the only damage they suffered will have been localized. An empty city will soon be reclaimed by nature, in the form of rodents and insects first, followed by weeds and vegetation. Roads should generally be useable and country areas and wildlife should be unaffected, and are the best place to begin a new settlement.

Threats will be limited, and will only be restricted to stray zombies that were infected at a very late stage (most likely survivors that failed). You may also come up against government remnants. These remnants may be in one of two situations. Either they consist of individuals who no longer have an official hierarchy or no chain of command and are just attempting to survive like you or they may have retained some form of rank or command structure but will have lost sight of their strategic or tactical objective. Units like this that have maintained cohesion will no doubt be ruled by a totalitarian officer. These are dangerous and should be avoided as they will still operate under the illusion of authority and treat survivors with a great deal of suspicion. Units like this will dissolve over time in tandem with the number of Zombies.

Other Apocalypses

Although the main apocalyptic scenarios have been covered, there are many more permutations and variations on the previous scenarios that may likely occur and require a different survival strategy. Fortunately many of these scenarios resemble those previously listed in terms of effects, detection and survival. In addition, there are cataclysmic afflictions that will destroy all life on earth without any chance of survival. These are listed below.

Vampiric Infection

Effects: Infected persons have a craving for blood and go into Vampiric coma during the day. Once a person is bitten, they too become afflicted and seek out other victims.

Detection: Spread of disease similar to spread patterns described in the 'Zombies' and 'Disease' chapter.

Survival: Survival should utilize principles described in 'Zombies' and 'Disease' chapter.

Volcanic Eruption

Effects: Previously dormant volcanoes explode with cataclysmic side effects. Earthquakes and tsunamis result on a global scale. Effects similar to those listed in 'Meteor'. Giant Earthquakes and Tsunamis also fit into this section.

Detection: Detection very short term similar in manner to those listed under them 'Meteor' section.

Survival: Survival should utilize principles described in 'Nuclear' and 'Meteor' sections.

Grey Goo

Effects: Self-replicating nano-machines absorb external cells to provide energy for further mutations, resulting in further endless replication. Consuming everything in their path, they replicate endlessly until they have consumed all life on earth, and the earth itself.

Detection: Detection would be a mixture of those listed in 'Artificial Intelligence' as well as 'Aliens'.

Survival: The only method for surviving such goo would be via the result of massive simultaneous nuclear detonations and resulting EMP pulses to destroy/incapacitate the replicating nano-machines. This would only work if it was enacted early enough and would result in serious side effects such as those listed in the 'Nuclear' chapter. Other than this, there is no survival option for Grey Goo as everywhere would be eventually consumed.

Mutant Insects

Effects: Through the introduction and eventual mutation of genetically modified crops insects mutate grotesquely into larger and more voracious creatures. Locusts, beetles and other flying insects start to devour crops and foods at an astounding rate and breeding at an even faster rate. This results in swarms of giant mutated insects laying siege to everything in their path.

Detection: Detection would be a mixture of those listed in the 'Aliens' chapter, as well as 'Zombies'.

Survival: Survival would be a combination of those listed in the 'Nuclear' chapter (living underground), the 'Aliens' chapter (on forming survivor communities) and the 'Zombies' chapter (on general survival). Starvation would be a major threat but insect numbers would eventually dwindle in tandem with food supplies.

Gamma Ray Burst

Effects: Caused by the merging of collapsed stars. If these were to occur anywhere near enough to earth (under 100 light years away) these would cause a powerful burst of gamma rays to penetrate the atmosphere, destroying our ozone layer completely due to the flooding of nitrogen oxides in the atmosphere. The resulting rays would cook plankton used to photosynthesize our oxygen and make the atmosphere unbreathable.

Detection: Detection is almost impossible, but in cosmic phenomenon would be similar to those listed in the 'Meteor' chapter.

Survival: Unless an underground shelter is built long beforehand with its own self sustained greenhouse, then survival is impossible. A lack of atmosphere would kill most animal and plant life and even underground survivors would quickly find themselves facing dehydration or starvation.

Black Holes

Effects: Another cosmic phenomenon caused by collapsed stellar bodies, creating an intense gravity on everything that surrounds them. The pull is in fact so intense that even light does not escape the gravity vortex that it generates, hence the name 'Black Hole'. If a Black Hole passed through our solar system then this would drastically affect the orbit of the earth. If it passed close enough it could easily swallow earth entirely and destroy it, or more realistically have detrimental effects on its orbit. Earth would either change orbit drastically, throwing into extreme climate changes or breaking its orbit completely and sending it towards or away from the sun. On a separate note, there is a theory among various academics that it is theoretically possible (although realistically impossible) to produce strangelets via a particle accelerator mishap, thereby causing the creation of a black hole right here on earth. In any case, the creation of a black hole on earth would make survival impossible.

Detection: Detection is almost impossible, but in cosmic phenomenon would be similar to those listed in the 'Meteor' chapter. Black Holes are typically located by sets of calculations designed to pinpoint it when stellar bodies in the vicinity begin to exhibit new previously unobserved orbits or gravity behavior.

Survival: Depending on the outcome of Earths encounter with a black hole, survival may be possible. Survival is impossible if Earth is sent towards the Sun, away from the Sun or is consumed by the Black Hole. If Earths orbit is affected by a more elliptical orbit then this will only result in wild climate changes, which while not earth destroying will cause ecological migration to parts of the planet that are more stable. Previous cities that had normal seasons will be abandoned due to rigors of the new climate.

Genetically Modified Crop mutation

Effects: Various genetically modified crops are produced to only serve a single generation, producing no seed and thereby having to have a new batch engineered every year. If such strains were to mutate and infect other foods, then this would cause a worldwide crop failure that would only produce a single generation of crop, with no further seeds.

Detection: Detection would be very different, but akin to those listed in the 'Disease' chapter.

Survival: Short term survival would equate in similar terms to those employed in the 'Disease' chapter. Long term survival would be extremely difficult without a food source, as all forms of crop would be destroyed. An option would be to forage so effectively as to survive on canned and non-perishable foods for as long as possible while the ecology recovers naturally.

Artificial Existence

Effects: After some kind of infrastructure failure, we are awoken to the rude shock that our existence has been a virtual one from our 'birth'. The world which we have been 'living' in is gone instantaneously.

Detection: Detection not possible, although the event may be preceded by unusually impossible activities by people around you (such as flying or walking through walls).

Survival: Mass insanity would no doubt result on a global scale. Although there are numerous factors to consider, the physical state of a body after a lifetime of gestation in a virtual world would be poor. It may ensue that only the brain remains and the body has been disposed of to facilitate the storage of the human population for this virtual existence. If this level of self-awareness were to occur, it would most likely produce insanity.

Death of magnetic core

Effects: The magnetic core at earth's center stops spinning or slows down too much. This causes a collapse of earths magnetic fields which protect earth from the harmful radiation from the Sun. Radiation from the Sun decimates crops, animals and dries up oceans as well as causing violent unstable super-storms.

Detection: Similar to the cosmic phenomenon detailed in the 'Meteor' chapter, including the violent earthquake phenomenon that follows.

Survival: Survival is not possible longer than short term as all life, including plant and animal would be destroyed. Water in all its forms would disappear alongside the oxygen rich atmosphere. The planet would eventually resemble our sister planet, Mars.

The Unknown Apocalypse

There are many other ways life could end on this planet before our time as its inhabitants cease. Many theories abound on when and how this will occur, but it is hard to shake the sinister tension that pervades on the state of the world today. Regardless of what cataclysmic event you find yourself in, certain principles will always hold true to aid your survival. In addition, there will always be only 3 things you require for survival: water, food and shelter. Without these, survival is not possible. In any event, follow the 3 below principles in order to ensure your long term survival:

1. Leave Cities and large population centers

2. Find a suitable shelter

3. Spend your days seeking food, water and other survivors

These are the basics of survival, and indeed will complement the basics of life. It is hoped that you will never endure any such fate, nor have to survive under any of the conditions described previously. Unfortunately it is a testament to the uncertainty of the world that we live in that we are forever on the brink of something new. We can never escape factors which we have no control over, such as those that emerge from the vast cosmos above or those inflicted upon us by our deities. However, the current state of society leaves much to debate on how we serve our fellow man. Community in its truest form has disappeared entirely, replaced by self-absorbed individuals working alongside each other, but ultimately for their own betterment. Relinquishing the culture of rights that we champion and replacing it with a culture of responsibility can only benefit everyone. We are human after all and all have our entrenched foibles that persist throughout our history and that we have to fight introspectively every day.

Edna St. Vincent Millay, the accomplished poet and author embodied these feelings when she said *"I love humanity but I hate people."*

The most insightful view into our human activity originates from the most brilliant mind of the 20th century, Albert Einstein. It is perhaps the mastery of his own mind that enabled him to grasp the human condition and give us direction in our tense world going forward:

"A human being is a part of the whole called by us universe, a part limited in time and space. He experienced himself, his thoughts and feeling as something separated from the rest, a kind of optical delusion of his consciousness. This delusion is a kind of prison for us, restricting us to our personal desires and to affection for a few persons nearest to us. Our task must be to free ourselves from this prison by widening our circle of compassion to embrace all living creatures and the whole of nature in its beauty."

Albert Einstein

Bibliography

Cardis, Elisabeth et al. 2006 'Cancer consequences of the Chernobyl
   accident: 20 years on'. *Journal of Radiological Protection. Issue no 2.(127-140)*

Kearny, Cresson H. 1987 *Nuclear War Survival Skills*

   Oregon Inst Science & Medicine, Cave Junction.

Lundin, Cody. 2003. 98.6 degrees – *The Art of Keeping Your Ass Alive*

   Gibbs Smith.

Forgey, William. 1991 W. *Basic Essentials of Hypothermia*. ICS Books.

Churchill, James E. 1991 *Basic Essentials of Survival*. ICS Books

Gonzales, Laurence. 2003. *Deep Survival – Who Lives, Who Dies and Why*.

   WW Norton & Company.

Lehman, Charles A. 1979. *Emergency Survival*. Primer Publishers

Stewert, Charles E. 1989. *Environmental Emergencies*. Williams & Wilkens

Shuh, Dwight R. 1979. *Modern Survival*. MCkay Press.

Davies, Barry BEM. 1999. *SAS Encyclopedia of Survival*. Virgin Publishing

   Limited.

Davies, Barry BEM. 1996. *The SAS Escape, Evasion & Survival Manual*.

   Motorbooks International.

Leach, John. 1994. *Survival Psychology*. New York University Press.

Wiseman, John. 1986. *The SAS Survival Handbook*. HarperCollins Pub.

Simpson, Joe. 1998. *Touching the Void*. HarperPerennial.

Dzugan, Jerry & Jensen, Susan Clark. 1999. *Water Wise*.

   USMSA University of Alasksa Sea Grant.

Reid, Piers P. 1974. *Alive*. Lippencot Press.

Segre, Emilio, 1980. *From X-Rays to Quarks: Modern Physicists and Their*

Discoveries. W. H. Freeman.

Beth, Hans A. 1991. *The Road from Los Alamos.* American Institute of
    Physics.

Schweber, Silvan S. 2000. *In the Shadow of the Bomb: Bethe, Oppenheimer, and
    the Moral Responsibility of the Scientist.* Princeton University Press.

Sherwin, Martin J. 2003. *A World Destroyed: Hiroshima and its Legacies.*
    Stanford University Press.

Caufield, Catherine. 1989. *Multiple Exposures: Chronicles of the Radiation Age.*
    University of Chicago.

Glasstone, Samuel and Philip J. Dolan. 1977. *The Effects of Nuclear
    Weapons.* 3d ed. US Government Printing Office.

Hansen, Chuck. 1988. *US Nuclear Weapons: The Secret History.*
    Orion Books.

Rosenberg, Howard L. 1980. *Atomic Soldiers: American Victims of Nuclear
    Experiments.* Beacon Press.

Taylor, Lauriston Sale. 1971. *Radiation Protection Standards.* CRC Press.

Yoshikawa, T. 1990. *Foundations of Robotics: Analysis and Control.* MIT Press.

Winston, P. H. 1992. *Artificial Intelligence.* Addison-Wesley.

Weizenbaum, J. 1976. *Computer Power and Human Reason.* W. H. Freeman.

Weld, D. and Etzioni, O. 1994. *The First Law of Robotics: A Call to Arms.*
    *In Proceedings of the Twelfth National Conference on Artificial
    Intelligence,*AAAI Press.

Boden, M. A. 1990. *The Philosophy of Artificial Intelligence.*
    Oxford University Press.

Charniak, E. and McDermott, D. 1985. *Introduction to Artificial Intelligence.*
    Addison-Wesley.

Copeland, J. 1993. *Artificial Intelligence: A Philosophical Introduction*. Blackwell

Crevier, D. 1993. *AI: The Tumultuous History of the Search for Artificial Intelligence*. Basic Books.

Dreyfus, H. L. 1972. *What Computers Can't Do: A Critique of Artificial Reason*. Harper and Row.

Dreyfus, H. L. 1992. *What Computers Still Can't Do: A Critique of Artificial Reason*. MIT Press.

Chan, P.K.S. et al. 2001 'Pathology of Fatal Infection Associated with Avian Influenza A H5N1 Virus.' *Journal of Medical Virology* 63, no. 3 (March), 242-46.

Collier, Richard. 1996. *America's Forgotten Pandemic.*Allison and Busby.

Frost, W.H. 1920. 'Statistics of Influenza Morbidity.' *Public Health Reports* 7 (12 March): 584-97.

Guerra, F. 1988. 'The Earliest American Epidemic: The Influenza of 1493.' *Social Science History* 12, no. 3: 305-25.

Hoehling, Adolph A. 1961. *The Great Epidemic*. Little Brown.

Iezzoni, Lynette. *Influenza 1918: The Worst Epidemic in American History*. TV Books, 1999.

Ranger, Terence and Paul Slack eds. 1992. *Epidemics and Ideas: Essays on the Historical Perceptions of Pestilence*. Cambridge University Press.

Barry, John M. 2004 *The Great Influenza: The Epic Story of the Deadliest Plague in History*. Viking Press.

Glezen, W.P. 1996 'Emerging Infections: Pandemic Influenza.' *Epidemiology Review* 18, no. 1: 64-76.

Cottrell, A., 1999, 'Sniffing the Camembert: on the Conceivability of
   Zombies', *Journal of Consciousness Studies,* 6: 4-12

Flanagan, O., and T. Polger, 1995, 'Zombies and the Function of
   Consciousness', *Journal of Consciousness Studies,* 2: 313-321.

Harnad, S., 1995, 'Why and How We Are Not Zombies', *Journal of
   Consciousness Studies* 1: 164-167

Marcus, E., 2004. 'Why Zombies are Inconceivable', *Australasian Journal of
   Philosophy* 82: 477-90

Tanney, J., 2004. 'On the Conceptual, Psychological, and Moral Status of
   Zombies, Swamp-Beings, and Other 'Behaviourally
   Indistinguishable' Creatures', *Philosophy and Phenomenological
   Research* 69: 173-86

Barkun, Michael. 1974. *Disaster and the Millennium.* Yale University Press.

Emmerson, Richard K., and Bernard McGinn, eds 1992.. *The Apocalypse in
   the Middle Ages.* Cornell University Press.

McGinn, Bernard, John J. Collins, and Stephen J. Stein, eds. 1998 *The
   Encyclopedia of Apocalypticism.* Continuum.

O'Leary, Stephen D. 1994. *Arguing the Apocalypse: A Theory of Millennial
   Rhetoric.* Oxford University Press.

Strozier, Charles B., and Michael Flynn. 1997. *The Year 2000: Essays on the
   End.* New York University Press.

Benware, Paul N. 1995. *Understanding the End Times: A Comprehensive
   Approach.* Moody Press.

Walvoord, John F. 1991. *Major Bible Prophecies.*
   Zondervan Publishing House.

Walvoord, John F.1990. *Armageddon, Oil and the Middle East*

Crisis..Zondervan Publishing House.

Lindsey, Hal. 1994. *Planet Earth-2000 A.D.* Western Front Ltd.

Jeffrey, Grant R. 1988. *Armageddon: Appointment with Destiny.*

    Frontier Research Publications.

Hocking, David. 1988. *The Coming World Leader.* Multnomah Press.

Biederwolf, William E. 1991 *The Prophecy Handbook.* World Bible

    Publishers.

Lalonde, Peter and Paul Lalonde. 1994. *The Mark of the Beast.*

    Harvest House Publishers.

Littmann, Mark and Yeomans, Donald K. 1985. *Comet Halley:*

    Once in a Lifetime. American Chemical Society.

Corliss, William R. 1983. *Tornados, Dark Days, Anomalous*

    Precipitation, and Related Weather Phenomena. The

    Sourcebook Project

Erickson, Jon. 1991. *Target Earth! Asteroid Collisions Past and Future.* Tab Books.

Hodge, Paul. 1994. *Meteorite craters and impact structures of the*

    Earth. Cambridge University Press

Norton, Richard O. 2002. *The Cambridge Encyclopedia of*

    Meteorites. Cambridge University Press

Printed in the United Kingdom
by Lightning Source UK Ltd.
126952UK00001B/255/A